Martin McMillan and the Lost Inca City

Elaine Russell

Illustrated by
Emily M D Cornell du Houx

Polar Bear & Company
Solon Maine U.S.A.

To my husband, Roy, and my son, Russell,
for their love and support.

Polar Bear & Company
P.O. Box 311, Solon, Maine 04979 U.S.A.
207 643-2795
www.polarbearandco.com

Illustrations and cover by Emily M D Cornell du Houx.
First edition. Manufactured in the U.S.A. by Thomson-Shore, Inc., an employee
owned company, using soy ink and acid free, recycled paper of archival
quality, at paper permanence specifications defined by ANSI.NISO standard
Z39.48-1992: "The ability of paper to last several hundred years without
significant deterioration under normal use and storage conditions in libraries
and archives."
Library of Congress Control Number: 2004100191
ISBN 1-882190-86-6

Contents

Martin McMillan
and the
Lost Inca City

Chapter 1

Upside Down

MARTIN McMILLAN TURNED off his Game Boy and gazed out the airplane window. It was hard to believe that two weeks ago life had seemed perfect. He'd been hanging out with the guys, skateboarding and talking about their first week in seventh grade. What a day! He'd finally landed that jump, after trying all summer. He remembered the vibration of the wheels spinning faster and faster as his left foot propelled the skateboard, how he'd held his breath, leaned to the right to avoid the bulging crack in the sidewalk, and headed straight up the sloping side of Mrs. Harris's one-foot cement wall. The trucks scraped noisily along the edge as he bent his knees and threw his weight into the jump. For a few fleeting seconds he sailed four feet into the air. The wheels hit the cement with a thud; the board rocked and twisted until he found his balance and finished with a one-eighty.

"Sweet," Charlie said, rushing over to give him a high five. Ryan and Trevor gave him thumbs up.

Only an hour later, still flushed with success, he'd raced back to the house to tell his parents. Then his world turned upside down. Dad met him on the porch. "Martin," he said, "I have the most exciting news."

Martin put his skateboard down and held his breath. He'd heard that one before. "What?"

"Your mother and I have been invited on a very important dig. We leave for Peru in two weeks." Dad had grinned and looked at him like he should be thrilled. Martin had run to his room and slammed the door.

Now he pounded the armrest with a fist as his jaw tensed. Every time he thought about what his parents were doing to him, his stomach curdled. It was so unfair! How could they make him leave his friends and miss his first year of junior high school, and for what—one of their stupid archaeological excavations? They made such a big deal about this amazing discovery that was so secret. Like he cared.

The family had left Chicago early that morning for Miami and a second flight to Lima, Peru. Just his luck to get parents who dragged him off to bug-infested jungles and barren deserts. Egypt had been the worst, but Thailand had sucked, too. In Peru there'd be another dirty camp with those disgusting smelly outhouses and no other kids, or at least none that spoke English.

Martin's life had never been normal until his family moved home to Silverton, Illinois, when he was ten. The last two years had been so cool, living with Grandma and having friends he didn't have to leave, or so he'd thought. Finally his parents had real jobs. Mom loved teaching at the University of Illinois, and Dad had been thrilled to get the curator position at the Museum of Natural History.

The same futile questions kept running over and over in his mind. *Why this? Why Peru?* Had Mom and Dad even thought about consulting him, or his sister, Jenny? No! All they had cared about was themselves.

He hoped his skateboard was okay. The airline had made him check it with the baggage at the last minute. If his new trucks and wheels got damaged, he'd be lost. What would he do in the middle of nowhere without his board?

Jenny, fifteen years old, slept in the seat next to him, her headphones pounding out the beat of Everclear. At least she wasn't throwing a tantrum. Martin had spent the past few weeks sulking and slamming doors. He'd even refused to pack his suitcase. But Jenny had screamed and sobbed nonstop, swearing that her parents were ruining her life. A lot of good any of it had done either one of them.

The captain of the plane announced their descent into Lima. Martin looked for the ground, but a sea of gray clouds blocked the view. Dad's head popped over the seat in front of Martin, and Mom stood in the aisle next to Jenny.

"Jenny, wake up, honey." Mom gently shook Jenny's shoulder. "We're going to be landing soon." Jenny opened her eyes and groaned as Mom took the headphones off her ears and pushed Jenny's tray back into the seat in front. "Anyone need to use the bathroom before we land?"

"Oh, Mother!" Jenny snapped as she tried to turn away.

There was nowhere to turn but into Martin's face. "Don't say anything, stupid."

Jenny was such a pain. She always took everything out on him. When he was little, she used to call him Spot, making fun of the freckles laced across his nose and cheeks. He looked like his dad, blond hair, blue eyes and freckles, while Jenny inherited Mom's auburn hair and brown eyes. Jenny used to make him so mad, but lately he'd found a way to turn the tables.

"Look who's talking, Spot!" Martin smiled, knowing how embarrassed she was about the zits that turned her face into a connect-the-dots puzzle.

"Stop it, you two!" Dad said frowning.

Mom seemed kind of excited and worried, all at the same time. She kept playing with her hair and straightening her jacket. Dad's face looked pale.

It took forty-five minutes to negotiate four suitcases and a large trunk through customs. They wound their way among anxiously waiting crowds who pushed and pulled in total chaos. Spanish and English announcements blared from the loud speakers, "Señor Martínez, please come to the Aero Perú counter." Families called out excitedly as passengers emerged from the gate.

"Hold on to your backpacks. You don't want to lose

anything," Mom warned Jenny and Martin for the third time. Her face relaxed when she caught sight of a man standing beyond the crowd, holding up a yellow sign—Wells Expedition.

A small, rotund man with a bushy beard and rosy cheeks waved and smiled. Martin thought he looked like Santa Claus, only with brown hair. Dr. Wells, the director of the expedition, had been Mom's advisor in graduate school.

"Amelia, my dear, how delightful to see you again," Dr. Wells said, pumping Mom's hand vigorously. "You remember my wife, Edna." Mrs. Wells stood two inches taller than her husband. Her auburn hair, streaked with gray, formed a loose bun at the nape of her neck. Something about her smile reminded Martin of Grandma.

"And this is your husband Harvey, of course," Dr. Wells continued.

"Yes. Very pleased to see you again," Dad said. "And these are our children, Jenny and Martin."

Jenny barely nodded and surveyed the terminal as if searching for someone.

Martin mumbled, "Hi."

"I can't wait for you to meet the other young people, eight of you in all, quite a group," Dr. Wells said. Martin looked up, surprised. Maybe there would be someone his age.

"As you probably know," Dr. Wells continued, "Mrs. Wells will be your teacher."

She smiled reassuringly.

"I'm sure once we get settled, they'll be very happy," Mom said, sharply directing her voice toward Jenny.

"One more family arrives this afternoon from Spain," Dr. Wells explained. "Tomorrow we have a slide presentation and the dinner with the Peruvian Ministry. Tuesday, we're off to Cajamarca and our camp."

"You must be exhausted," Mrs. Wells said, patting Mom's

arm. "We have a van out front to take you to the hotel. We'll leave you on your own this evening."

Martin peered out the van windows into the fading light of day as they sped to the center of Lima. The outskirts of town appeared flat and gray. Dilapidated shacks peppered abandoned lots overgrown with weeds. Barefoot children played by the side of the road. As they arrived downtown, traffic slowed to a crawl, and the crowded streets bustled with activity. Dark-skinned men and women in brightly colored clothes packed the sidewalks with their wares—candy, papers, toys and jewelry—arrayed on makeshift stands. The air hung thick with brown smog, turning the sky an eerie orange, as the last rays of sunlight peeked through clouds. Martin thought it looked like the foreign cities he had seen before—Istanbul, Bangkok, Cairo—too many people living in one place and most of them poor. What would life be like in this strange land?

Chapter 2

New Faces

THE NEXT AFTERNOON the excavation team crowded into the hotel conference room and sat facing a projection screen. Dr. Wells stood at the podium, adjusting slides in the projector, his face flushed with excitement.

Martin glanced around the room. A girl about his age sat erect in the front row, a mass of unruly gold hair flowing down her back. She turned and met his gaze, and he looked away.

"Stop pushing your brother!" One row back, Martin watched an extremely chubby kid shove his younger brother. The father grabbed the older boy's arm and pulled him into the seat next to him. "Honestly, Josh, you act like you're three years old." Josh crossed his arms, his face turning red.

Next to Martin, Jenny slumped in her seat, with a perpetual scowl. He could see her eyes darting about, assessing the crowd.

From the back of the room, a family burst through the doors, speaking rapidly in a language he didn't recognize. There were twin boys, maybe six or seven, and a teenage boy who scooted down the row to the seat next to Jenny. He had wavy black hair and long lashes that drooped over huge brown eyes. He gave Jenny a lopsided smile. She sat up and smoothed her hair behind her ears.

When everyone settled, Dr. Wells began, "I want to welcome you to the expedition. This team represents the best expertise in our field, and we are thrilled to have you." He surveyed the group with a pleased smile. "I'd like to give some background on the project and the task ahead."

Dr. Wells described the different groups that had lived in Peru prior to the Incas. Martin shifted in his seat. How long was this boring talk going to last? Half listening, he watched a series of slides flash upon the screen with drawings of early civilizations, ornate golden masks, and earthen pottery. They looked like the things he'd seen at the Museo de la Nación that morning. *What a waste of time!*

He had gotten up early to ride his skateboard around Lima, but as he was leaving, his parents had intercepted him. They refused to let him go out alone. He didn't get it. He could take care of himself. Instead they insisted he go to the museum with them, even though they let Jenny stay in bed. To make matters worse, they wanted to tell him about every statue and pot in the museum in excruciating detail. Deadly! He had ended up playing his Game Boy in the museum lobby for an hour, waiting for Mom and Dad.

Dr. Wells's voice rose with enthusiasm. "As you may know, the Incas, or Quechuas, started as a small ethnic group in the Andes Mountains. Inca means 'lord' in the Quechua language. Over time, the people came to be known by this name. Quechua is still spoken by many of the native people in the Andes. But many speak Spanish as well, like the people in the village near our camp."

Martin felt his eyes drooping with the monotonous tone of Dr. Wells's voice. He pulled out his Game Boy, but Mom glanced over, frowned, and shook her head, no. He looked at her with disbelief. What did she expect him to do?

A brightly colored map of South America appeared on the screen as Dr. Wells picked up a pointer. "Throughout the fourteenth and fifteenth centuries, the Incas built the most amazing empire, conquering neighbors on all sides and taking control of one third of South America." He stroked his beard. "They built fantastic cities and temples, feats of architecture. The land was rich with gold and silver. They used it everywhere—for jewelry, sculpture and artwork. Imagine! They even covered their walls in gold!"

Jenny appeared to listen intently, periodically glancing at the boy next to her. Martin could guess why she was suddenly interested in the project. She kept flipping her long hair over her shoulders. She was *so dumb*.

"Over time, the Incas lost their hold over the empire," Dr. Wells continued. "In 1532, the arrival of the Spanish conquistadors, led by Francisco Pizarro, ended the Incas' rule. Overwhelmed by greed for gold and silver, the Spanish killed the Inca emperor and many of his people. A very sad episode in history, indeed."

Martin wondered which family was from Spain and if they felt badly. But it had been a long time ago. It wasn't really their fault.

Dr. Wells pointed to a spot on a map of Peru. "Our excavation site is here, by the little village of Jalca, which means 'lofty region' in Quechua. It's located about two hundred miles northeast of Lima. I discovered the site on my last expedition quite by accident. We believe it may be the lost city Karu Orq'o, which means 'far mountain' in Quechua. The only reference made to Karu Orq'o was found in a letter written in 1549 by Spanish conquistador Don José Carlos Mendoza. He wrote his brother in Spain of a secret city hidden in the mountains, filled with great treasures, temples overflowing with gold, silver and jewels. Mendoza died shortly after this and no one ever discovered the city again."

Dr. Wells leaned on the podium, peered over his glasses, and spoke in a hushed voice, "Some in the field believe Mendoza found Machu Picchu, but I hope we have another story to tell."

A picture of steep, forested mountains appeared on the screen. Dr. Wells continued, "The site is tucked away in a valley hidden behind these mountains, surprisingly, a considerable way off the Old Inca Trail. The area is overgrown with thick forests and vines. You can see how it could be easily overlooked. We literally tripped over a stone wall buried except for two inches jutting above ground." He explained that without permits they had only been able to take a few samples of stone back for analysis. The remnants were identified as being from the Inca period.

Mom took Dad's hand and squeezed it as they smiled at one another. Martin could feel their excitement. He had to admit, they loved their work. But that didn't change anything; he was still mad at them.

The young boy behind Martin squirmed in his chair and said loudly, "When is this going to be over, Mommy? I'm bored."

Laughter rippled through the room. Dr. Wells cleared his throat and ruffled through his notes. "Well, I think we'll end here. I want to quickly introduce our team. If you could stand and say 'hoo hoo' as I call your name."

Josh snickered loudly and Martin couldn't help laughing too.

"First it's a great pleasure to introduce our esteemed colleague from Peru, Dr. Pablo Arturo, an expert on Inca sites. Next we have Dr. Carmen García, a professor of geology from the University of Madrid in Spain, and her daughter Isabel." The girl in the front row and her mother stood.

"Over here, Sara Bassett, our program administrator," Dr. Wells continued. "Then Drs. Amelia Hobbs, our field director, and Harvey McMillan from Chicago—one of our husband and wife duos—and their children, Martin and Jenny." Martin's face grew warm as his mother pulled his arm and made him stand.

"Here we have our wonderful photographer, Gino Bertolli from Florence, Italy, with his wife Louisa, his sons Paolo, and the twins, Mario and Roberto." Paolo winked at Jenny.

"Over here Drs. Henry and Lori Wilson from California with Josh and Andy." Josh had made a paper airplane from the agenda and threw it now at Andy, hitting him in the arm. Andy tried to reach over to hit Josh as their parents intervened.

"Dr. James Leonard, my assistant for fifteen years, is already at the site with our three young graduate students, making ready for our arrival. I know you probably have questions, but in the interest of not boring the children, we'll break for tea and cookies. Don't forget, 7:00 p.m. for our reception and dinner." Dr. Wells straightened his papers.

After a round of applause, a low murmur filled the room. Mom walked over to shake hands with Dr. García, and Dad studied a packet of information that had been passed out. Martin made for the back of the room. As he reached out for a cookie, Josh shoved him out of the way and grabbed four sugar cookies.

"Josh! Don't make a pig of yourself." Josh's father stood behind them, glaring.

Josh's face stiffened. He threw the cookies on the table, stomped out and slammed the door. His father ran after him.

Josh was a big kid, no doubt about it, half a foot taller than Martin and probably twice the weight. But it seemed pretty mean of his dad to embarrass him that way.

Martin was finishing his second cookie as Mrs. Wells approached with the girl from the front row.

"Martin, this is Isabel García-Hoffman," Mrs. Wells said.

"Hello," Isabel smiled and put her hand out to shake his.

Flustered, Martin extended a hand covered with cookie crumbs. "Hi." He felt himself blush as he stared into Isabel's bright green eyes. A mass of curls the color of caramel syrup fell around her face. All he could think of was Grandma's cat, Ginger.

"Isabel and her mother will be riding with your family to the site on Thursday," Mrs. Wells said. "You'll have a chance to get to know each other better. You're both twelve, and I know you'll have a lot in common."

What in the world could he have in common with a girl, especially one from Spain? Martin didn't know a lot of girls besides his sister and her friends, but if Isabel was anything like them, he wanted to stay clear.

Chapter 3

Into the Jungle

"**A**LL RIGHT, TEAM, I think we're ready," Dr. Wells called out. "We must get under way. It's going to be a long day of driving." He rushed about, herding people into cars and inspecting trunks filled with excavation equipment, suitcases, sleeping bags, dishes, pots, pans and basic food supplies.

The expedition team had flown from Lima to the highlands town of Cajamarca two days ago. Dr. Wells told them Cajamarca meant "region of rocks" in Quechua, and Martin thought it was a pretty good description. The brown rocky peaks of the Andes Mountains surrounded the city. They had spent one day touring the historic old town where Francisco Pizarro had tricked the last Inca emperor Atahuallpa into a trap.

Now the group gathered for the long drive to the remote site that would be their home for the next year. Each car had been given a map and instructions in case they lost track of the others in the caravan.

Martin checked his watch for the hundredth time and sighed. They had been scheduled to leave at 7:00 a.m., but it was already 8:30. He waited with his parents and Jenny in front of the hotel. Jenny waved to Paolo who smiled back from two cars away. She had spent every free minute over the last two days with him, giggling and batting her eyes. *How stupid!*

"When are we ever going to leave?" Martin asked. His feet hurt, and the early morning Sun did nothing to warm him.

"Just a few more minutes," Dad answered. "All the cars are packed now."

Martin's stomach grumbled. "I'm starving." They had gotten up so early, all he had eaten for breakfast was a hard roll and hot chocolate.

Mom pulled a banana from her purse. "I told you to eat more at breakfast."

He shrugged, "I wasn't hungry then."

Mom raised her eyebrows toward Martin and Jenny. "I believe a number of people are making a last bathroom stop. Any takers?"

"Oh, Mother," Jenny huffed as she left for the hotel ladies' room.

"Hey, wouldn't it be funny if Jenny came out and we were gone?" Martin suggested as he stuffed half a banana in his mouth. Mom and Dad gave him withering looks. They never appreciated his sense of humor.

"Go ahead and get in," Mom sighed. "I'll tell Carmen and Isabel we're ready to go."

Martin climbed into the van and took the far back seat. He placed his backpack on the floor at his feet. It contained his

important worldly possessions—Game Boy and games, a full box of batteries, the two latest skateboarding magazines, three new books, a sketchpad, colored pencils, a notebook from Grandma, and two finger skateboards from Charlie. But most important of all, his helmet and skateboard were in the back of the van.

Isabel peeked around the car door, inspecting the available seats. "Is it all right if I come back there?"

"Ah . . . yeah, sure," Martin stammered. *Oh great!* He had successfully avoided her for the last two days, but now he'd have to talk to her.

Martin had never gone to school with girls until he moved back to Silverton. He didn't know how to talk to them. Why were they always whispering and giggling and sending notes around the room? Life had shifted slightly the last few months of sixth grade. His friends started acting differently around the girls, trying to be cool and telling dumb jokes. They had quit saying how stupid girls were. It had been hard for Martin to figure out.

Isabel slid in among the seats to join him. She had a backpack and a long, zippered nylon bag which she carefully stowed at her feet. They watched as others climbed into cars.

He glanced at her. The silence stretched between them until he felt compelled to speak, "Can you believe all the stuff we're bringing?"

"Yes. This is the nearest city to our camp, where we can buy important things, but it's an eight-hour drive. My mother said someone will be driving here for supplies once a month." She gazed at him with her green eyes, serious and unwavering.

"Wow, I hope I don't have to go. I hate driving. Sometimes I get carsick."

She frowned and scrunched into the corner away from him. She gently tucked her things farther under the seat.

"What's in there?" he nodded toward her nylon bag.

"The new scooter my dad sent me." Her voice filled with excitement, "It's so fun."

"Cool. I'd love to have one of those, but my mom says I get into enough trouble with my skateboard." He eyed the bag as if the scooter might suddenly pop out. "I brought it—my skateboard, that is." He pointed behind them.

"Good. We could skate together. My mother doesn't think there'll be anywhere to ride, but I'm sure we can find someplace."

"Great." Martin thought a moment. "Where does your dad live?"

"San Francisco. He's a Spanish professor at U.C. Berkeley." She stared down at her feet. "He used to live in Spain, but my parents divorced when I was five."

"Sorry." He hesitated, unsure what to say. That explained why she spoke English so well.

"It's okay. I go back and forth each year between Spain and California. This year I'm with my mother, so I got to come here." She brushed a stray strand of hair from her forehead.

"Don't you miss your friends and stuff?"

She gave him an inquisitive look. "A little. But I like meeting new people and going different places."

He raised his eyebrows. "I hated leaving my friends and my grandmother. I didn't want to come at all."

"I have lots of friends in Spain and California, but time passes quickly. In a short while, we will be back." Isabel glanced out the window.

Just then Carmen García climbed into the middle seat, flashing a brilliant smile at Isabel and Martin. Her long dark hair, laced with strands the color of red wine, fell about her face and neck like a tiger's mane. Big brown eyes dominated her face. She had long legs and arms. In her jeans and sweatshirt, Martin thought she looked more like a teenager than someone's mom. He listened fascinated as she rattled on in Spanish to Isabel.

"Sí, Mamá." Isabel looked at Martin. "She has snacks for us, if we want them later."

Martin grinned. "Great. I'm hungry." Carmen laughed and handed him a bag of potato chips.

Jenny ran from the hotel and jumped in next to Carmen. Mom sat in the driver's seat as Dad studied the map in the seat next to her.

"Hooray! We're off at last," Mom called out.

"I don't know why I couldn't ride with Paolo," Jenny grumbled.

"Don't start that again," Mom snapped.

Jenny opened her backpack, pulled out her CD player, and slouched down in the seat to escape under her headphones. Isabel did the same.

Martin sighed and wished he hadn't lost his CD player at the skate park in Chicago last month. He put his head against the window and watched the center of town merge into rundown stores and small adobe and stone houses. As they reached the outskirts of Cajamarca, houses gave way to decaying shacks, and paved streets became dirt roads. A man in sandals, wearing a colorful poncho and a strange basket-shaped hat, walked by the side of the road with a donkey loaded with baskets of corn. Green hills stretched before them, spotted with llamas grazing contentedly. Steep, terraced fields melted into the jagged peaks of the Andes looming on the horizon. Martin's eyes grew heavy as he slowly drifted off to sleep.

* * *

Late in the afternoon the caravan switched back and forth around hairpin turns, creeping down a steep dirt path, the tires barely hanging on to their tenuous hold. Martin couldn't look down the sheer mountainside that fell straight below them. His stomach felt queasy, and his head hurt. He pushed the window out farther to let the cool fresh air rush over his face. Isabel seemed unperturbed, but Martin noticed Dr. García tense up as they rounded the turns.

The team had spent the first half of the day climbing steadily along a winding, rutted road. Martin and Isabel had played with their Game Boys, trading games periodically and discussing tactics. She had gone four levels farther than he had on his Super Mario.

Lunch had been a brief picnic followed by another hour climbing to the mountain peak. For three hours they descended into a narrow valley. The light grew dim, and shadows widened as the forest became dense with trees and vines. The temperature dropped at least twenty degrees in the last half hour. Across the valley, the fading sunlight reflected off barren granite cliffs.

"Dad, when are we going to get there?" Martin called to the front.

"Well, it's a little hard to say, but I think we must be close." Dad turned. "According to the map, we turn right at the bottom of the valley, and it's a few hundred yards."

After three more terrifying turns, the path straightened and leveled out. They had reached the valley floor. Five minutes later the lead car pulled over by a meadow. Martin glimpsed a series of adobe and stone buildings with pointed tile roofs stretching down a dirt road. A group of children from the village gathered, some jumping and waving, others hiding their faces shyly. A lanky boy leaned against the side of a tree, observing the arriving party. As Martin stepped out of the van, their eyes met, and the boy smiled. Martin nodded awkwardly.

On the far side of the meadow, a small village of tents and

cabins had been erected next to a stream. Several people stepped into view and walked toward them.

"Those must be the graduate students and Dr. Leonard," Dad said.

Jenny stared at their new surroundings, her eyes wide. "This is it?" she moaned. "You've got to be kidding."

Chapter 4

Questionable Roommates

JOSH STOOD OPPOSITE Martin in the middle of the small cabin with a wary look. His hulking body dwarfed the space. He threw his backpack on the first cot to the right. "I want this one," he said, his eyes narrowing.

"Okay," Martin shrugged his shoulders. He couldn't see what difference it made.

All four cots were exactly the same. The first bed on the left was occupied by one of the graduate students, Pete. He put his things down on the cot kitty-corner from Josh and hoped Paolo wouldn't mind taking the last spot.

Martin had been surprised by the assignment of cabins. He didn't mind; only the little kids were rooming with their parents. Being with the older guys could be fun, kind of like going to summer camp, which he'd never done. He did wonder about Josh who had mostly ignored him for the last few days and at times had been downright rude. He couldn't understand why.

Josh flopped down onto his cot. "What a dump."

Martin examined the rough floor built three feet off the ground and still smelling of freshly cut wood. Plastic pipes fit together like puzzle pieces to form a frame supporting canvas tenting. A single kerosene lamp hung from the center. In addition to the cots, two folding canvas chairs and a small metal table occupied the tent. Two large plastic storage bins had been placed under each bed.

"It's kind of bare," Martin admitted. "I guess we'll be spending most of our time outside or in the dining tent."

"This place is totally stupid. At least my dumb little brother is with my parents. They're always so worried about their precious little baby." Josh rolled his eyes.

Martin searched for common ground. "Do you have a Game Boy?"

"Why?"

"I thought maybe we could play and trade games."

"Well, I don't let anybody touch my stuff. Got it?"

"Yeah. Don't worry. I was just trying—oh, never mind." Martin turned to unpack his things into the plastic bins.

Dr. Wilson popped into the cabin with a suitcase for Josh. "I hope there isn't any trouble in here." He looked at Martin.

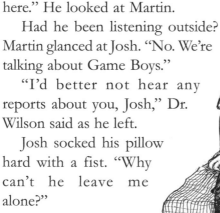

Had he been listening outside? Martin glanced at Josh. "No. We're talking about Game Boys."

"I'd better not hear any reports about you, Josh," Dr. Wilson said as he left.

Josh socked his pillow hard with a fist. "Why can't he leave me alone?"

Before Martin could think of anything to say, Paolo entered the cabin. "Hey, how is? This my bed?"

Martin loved listening to Paolo's halting English, which he spoke without the least bit of shyness. He was a nice, friendly guy. The only thing Martin couldn't figure out was why he seemed to like Jenny so much. What was there to like about his sister?

"Is that bed okay with you?" Martin asked. "I could trade if you want."

"I'm not trading," Josh snapped.

"No—is okay. You like music? I have nice player." Paolo held out his portable CD/tape player.

"Just don't play it when I'm here. I don't want to hear any dumb Italian music." Josh grabbed his sweatshirt and stormed out of the cabin.

"Man, what's wrong with that guy?" Martin said, shaking his head.

"Is too bad. He not happy. But we have good time, yes?" Paolo slapped Martin on the back so hard he nearly knocked him over. "Come. We eat dinner."

*   *   *

To Martin's relief, a remote satellite installed at the top of the mountain connected the camp with the outside world. After dinner his dad took him to the communications tent and showed him how to log onto the Internet.

Thursday, September 14th

Dear Grandma,
We're finally here at camp and it's way the heck far from anything. There's a village and a lot of trees and rocks. Not much else. Dad says we're just above the Amazon rainforest.

I'm sharing a tent with three guys. Jenny is in a cabin with the other girls. There is one big tent that's the dining hall and schoolroom where we can read and stuff. Tonight we had a big welcoming dinner with rice, beans, corncakes, salsa and mango. One of the ladies from the village did the cooking. Everything was pretty good.

Mom and Dad are really excited to be here and start working. I'm not as excited to start school

but Mrs. Wells seems like a nice lady so maybe it won't be too bad.

I'll write next week. I already finished the cookies you gave me when we left. They were great. Thanks.
Love, Martin (XOXOXO)

Martin paused a moment, thinking about what to tell Charlie. Not much had happened yet. A smile came over his face as he began to work the keyboard.

Hey Charlie,
We finally made it to our camp. What a drive getting to this place! I thought I was going to hurl for sure.

There are only two kids my age, this girl Isabel who is okay and Josh who has been a real jerk. Every time I try to talk to him, he just walks away. I'm beginning to think I have B.O. or something. I don't know what his problem is. I wish you could see this guy Dr. Leonard. He has a bald head and looks exactly like Dr. Evil in Austin Powers. Weird. He's pretty nice except he tells dumb jokes.

School starts tomorrow and my parents can't wait to go to the site to start work. Life is going to be so boring here. Help! Wish you could come visit. Why don't you ask your parents if you could come at Christmas? That would be tight. I'll write soon. Martin

Chapter 5

Pedro

MARTIN WOKE TO the sound of a bird squawking loudly on the top of the tent.

Pete rolled over, threw his tennis shoe, and grunted, "Scram." The thud on the canvas sent the bird into flight. A rooster crowed and another answered.

Martin slipped out of his sleeping bag. Cold air sent shivers down his back. He threw on his jeans, sweatshirt and sneakers. He wanted to look around before everyone woke up. After a quick stop at one of the outhouses, he washed his hands in a bucket of cold water. He strolled along the stream's edge, watching water bubble between rocks and small fish scour the shallow bottom.

"Hi."

Martin started and turned. Isabel stood a few feet away. She wore jeans and a navy blue sweatshirt with University of California Berkeley in gold letters. Her thick hair was tied back in a loose braid.

"I thought I was the only one up so early," Martin said.

"I couldn't sleep. I thought I'd take a look around." Isabel's scooter was strapped across her back. "Do you want to come?"

"Sure. I'll grab my skateboard."

They set off across the meadow to the dirt road that ran through the village.

"How's your cabin?" Isabel asked.

"Okay. Paolo and Pete are really nice." Martin decided not to mention Josh.

"I'd rather be with my mother, but she's sharing a cabin with Sara Bassett." Isabel was with the graduate students, Carey and Samantha, and Jenny. "I like your sister a lot."

"Why?" Martin made a face. "She's a pain."

Isabel smiled. "I'd like to have a sister or brother."

"Go ahead. Feel free to take mine," Martin offered.

They reached the small houses in Jalca where families stirred. Smoke drifted from oven chimneys, and the smell of food made Martin's stomach growl. Several women stood at their open doors, smiling and nodding.

Martin and Isabel rounded a bend in the road. "Wow, I didn't think the village was this big," he said.

A square stone plaza spread before them, surrounded on three sides by rows of houses and a small church. On the fourth side of the square, three ladies sold potatoes, corn and other vegetables from wooden carts. The road continued on past the plaza, sloping down a slight hill.

Martin and Isabel followed a group of men wearing wide-brimmed cowboy hats. They filed down the road, carrying hoes and machetes. Martin spotted the boy who had been standing next to the tree when they arrived the day before. He walked ahead of them with a hoe. His broad, brown face turned toward them, and he smiled, waiting for Martin and Isabel to catch up.

Isabel greeted him, *"Hola."*

Martin knew this meant "hello" and mumbled the same, listening as Isabel and the boy spoke rapidly in Spanish.

Isabel turned to Martin. "This is Pedro. He's fifteen. He works with his father in the fields in the morning and goes to school in the afternoon at the church," she reported. "They live back there on the plaza."

"Great." Martin wondered how Isabel managed to get so much information from such a short conversation. He thought Pedro looked younger than fifteen. A few inches taller than Martin, his body was slim but sturdy. He wore blue jeans and a yellow t-shirt. "Tell him I wish I could speak Spanish."

"Don't worry; you'll pick it up," Isabel said.

Pedro ran his hand over the back of Martin's skateboard, his dark eyes full of admiration. He rambled on to Isabel.

"Pedro owns a skateboard. Can you believe it?" Isabel laughed. "His father brought it back from Lima last year."

Martin gave Pedro a thumbs-up. "Ask him if there's anywhere we can ride."

More conversation followed. Pedro hesitated, shaking his head, no. He walked behind Isabel, examining her scooter. He seemed to think for a minute, then smiling, he spoke again.

"Pedro says he'll show us a place this afternoon. We can meet him back here at four," Isabel translated.

"Gracias." Martin used one of the other words he knew— thank you. He held his hand up to Pedro for a high five, but Pedro looked confused. Isabel demonstrated. Pedro laughed and slapped Martin's hand.

Pedro left, calling out, *"¡Adios!* Goodbye!" He hurried to catch up with the men heading for their fields.

Isabel looked at Martin. "Pedro says we can't tell anyone that we're going with him. It's a secret place. Where do you suppose it could be?"

Chapter 6

Troublemaker

AFTER MEETING PEDRO, Martin and Isabel returned to camp for breakfast and their first day in class. The eight students gathered in the dining tent, seated at the long wooden tables and benches. Mrs. Wells positioned a whiteboard at one end next to a stack of textbooks.

"Welcome to your first day," Mrs. Wells began. "This morning I'm going to give you a test to determine your math and reading levels." They all groaned. "It won't take more than thirty minutes. But first let's get to know one another better."

She asked each of them to talk about their lives at home and what they liked to do for fun. Finally she asked them what they would miss most. That was easy for Martin—Charlie, Ryan, Trevor and Grandma.

Josh refused to participate. He scowled at the group, his

arms crossed, while Mrs. Wells ignored him. Martin wondered why he had to act so weird.

After lunch Mrs. Wells announced, "I'm going to divide you into three levels." Mario, Roberto and Andy, all seven years old, were sent to one table.

"Paolo and Jenny, you'll work together," continued Mrs. Wells. Jenny beamed as Paolo scooted closer. "Then we have Isabel, Martin and Josh as our middle group."

"I don't want to be with those guys," Josh blurted out from the far corner, turning red. "I should be with Jenny and Paolo. I'm thirteen and a lot smarter than anybody."

"We can talk about it later, Josh. You'll start out as I suggested," Mrs. Wells said calmly.

Josh slumped over the table on his chubby arms, his eyes narrowing to slits. He looked like he wanted to hit someone.

"Each day we'll start with a half hour of Spanish as a group." Mrs. Wells smiled at Isabel. "Isabel has offered to help me teach, so we can break off into smaller groups the second half hour. I expect you to be fluent in Spanish by the time we leave Jalca next year."

That couldn't be soon enough, thought Martin. The usual stuff—math, reading and spelling—and it would be as boring as ever. Maybe learning Spanish wouldn't be so bad. Then he could talk to Pedro.

Mrs. Wells made assignments and gave them the rest of the afternoon to read and do homework. Josh scribbled on a piece of paper for a few minutes, slammed his math book shut and stomped out. Martin noticed Mrs. Wells sigh and shake her head gently. Josh was turning out to be a bigger pain than Jenny.

Once school ended, Martin and Isabel sat by the stream next to camp, skipping stones and waiting for four o'clock to meet Pedro. Isabel's stone sailed over the water in five smooth jumps. Martin threw a stone two skips. Frustrated, he glanced up. "Dr. Wilson's going in the communications tent."

"Maybe he's sending a note to the ministry in Lima about the site," Isabel suggested.

"I thought that was Dr. Arturo's job." Martin picked up a small flat rock and smiled as it glided over the water in four bounces.

In a few minutes, Dr. Wilson emerged from the tent. He spotted them and stopped for a few seconds, as if thinking of something to say. Then he stomped off toward the excavation site.

"He always looks so mad. I wonder why?" Isabel said and checked her watch again.

"I don't know, but he sure is mean to Josh. It doesn't seem fair when he's so nice to Andy."

"My mom says Andy has asthma, and his parents worry about him."

"Hey guys," Dr. Leonard appeared suddenly, walking in their direction, "how was school today?"

Martin shrugged, "Okay."

"You couldn't have a better teacher. Mrs. Wells is wonderful." Dr. Leonard rolled up the sleeves on his oxford shirt. "I came back to camp to get something, but how about a quick game of soccer?"

Isabel glanced at her watch. "Thanks, but we're going to see a boy we met in the village this morning."

"That's great. Getting to know the locals is the best way to experience a country." Dr. Leonard ran a hand over his bald head, glistening in the hot Sun. "We'll play soccer another day. Have fun." He headed for the communications tent.

"It's almost four. We better go," Isabel said.

"Okay." Martin turned toward Isabel. "Maybe we should tell Mrs. Wells we're leaving."

"No. We promised Pedro to keep it secret."

Martin's parents had warned him not to wander off without informing someone in camp. "But what if something happens, and they don't know where we are?"

"Don't be silly." Isabel flipped her long braid over her shoulder. "What could happen?"

Chapter 7

The Secret Path

PEDRO WAITED FOR Martin and Isabel in the same spot, but slightly out of view behind a tree. He called softly to them, holding a battered skateboard that looked so old Martin didn't know how he could ride it.

"Hey, Pedro!" Martin called out, waving.

Pedro put a hand up to be quiet and glanced around cautiously. He whispered to Isabel.

"He says we have to be very quiet and follow closely," Isabel translated in a hushed voice.

Off in the distance three men weeded a terraced field, unaware of the friends meeting below. It amazed Martin how much land could be planted on what looked like giant steps running up the steep mountainside.

Martin and Isabel trailed after Pedro, winding through the trees. Bushes and vines grew thicker, making it hard to continue. The light grew dim, and branches brushed their arms and legs.

Something pierced Martin's leg, "Ouch!"

Pedro put a finger to his mouth.

Martin cringed. "Are there any snakes in here?" he whispered. He was afraid to look down, afraid he'd see a giant snake attached to his leg, some deadly, poisonous, green snake. Suddenly, he felt light headed and short of breath. He slowly lowered his eyes to his thigh. It was only a thorny vine stuck to his pants. He pulled it free and moved on.

They approached a huge, gnarled tree trunk with roots that spread twenty feet across. Overhead, tree limbs formed an enormous umbrella. Thick vines with tiny teardrop leaves hung off the branches, creating a solid curtain that fanned out to the edge of the mountainside. Pedro motioned to stop.

Isabel glanced at Martin. Did he see a touch of uncertainty in her eyes, or was he the only one feeling funny? This was kind of creepy.

Pedro glanced to both sides and behind them, then put his hand into the vines at the base of the tree and pulled them back to create a small opening. He nodded for Martin and Isabel to step through.

"Go ahead," Martin whispered to Isabel.

She cocked her head. "You're not afraid, are you?"

"Of course not."

Isabel stooped low and slipped out of sight. Martin wondered why Pedro kept looking around. Who did he think might be following them? But he couldn't back out now. He took a deep breath, pushed his skateboard in front of him and ducked down. His head and body popped out the other side as he tripped over a root, nearly landing on his face. Pedro appeared immediately behind him and the curtain closed.

A winding path stretched before them with smooth square stones precisely laid together, flat and seamless. To the right, trees and plants formed a dense thicket, while sheer granite cliffs loomed above them on the left. The path followed the base of the valley floor along the mountain. Martin had an eerie feeling that they didn't belong here.

Pedro whispered to Isabel again. "He says, if we go a little farther, we can start riding," Isabel repeated.

"What is this place?" Martin said softly. "Do you think it's part of the ancient city?"

"Maybe—" Isabel glanced around. "But the excavation site is in the other direction."

After few more minutes, Pedro let Isabel know they could start riding.

Despite the nervous feeling in his stomach, Martin couldn't contain his excitement at the thought of flying along the path on his skateboard. "This is cool!"

Pedro turned and smiled. He may not have understood Martin's words, but it was clear he had caught the enthusiasm in his voice. "Ask him why this is such a big secret," Martin said to Isabel. "I don't get it."

Isabel and Pedro talked. "I'm not sure I understand," Isabel said. "He says this is a special place for his village, something religious. They don't want Dr. Wells to find out about it, so we can't tell our parents. We have to promise."

Martin shrugged his shoulders. "That's cool. If we told them, we'd probably get stuck here another year."

Isabel smiled and shook her head. She unfolded her scooter and pulled up to lock the handles in place. Pedro watched with interest. She stepped on and gave a push, rolling down the stones. "Come on, you guys!"

Pedro nodded at Martin, and they jumped on their skateboards. Pedro rode with incredible skill, jumping, kicking and grinding off rocks and logs along the path—a perfect heal flip, then an ollie. Martin wondered if Pedro had any idea what these moves were called. How had he learned them? Isabel soared along at amazing speed, jumping up and spinning around. She was good. The road wound around trees, creating exciting twists and bumps.

"This is tight!" Martin yelled to his friends.

Fifteen minutes into the ride, the road ended, and the stones

expanded into a large square, much like the plaza in the village. In the center, Martin saw a gold face, or maybe it was a mask, surrounded by squiggly lines radiating out in all directions.

Isabel's puzzled eyes met Martin's. "What's this?"

Pedro explained quickly that an old temple lay beyond the square, but they could go no farther. He held his skateboard, twirling the front wheel, as his eyes darted around the plaza. Suddenly he told Isabel they needed to go back to the village right away.

As Isabel and Pedro started off, Martin noticed his shoelace had come untied. He called out, "Hey, guys, wait for me!" They continued to roll back toward the path.

Squatting to tie his laces, he listened to the high-pitched cacophony of birds chirping and trilling. He pulled hard on a double knot as a flicker of white from the trees caught his eye. He stood and spun around. Nothing. Maybe a parrot had flown between branches. He had seen them before, high in the canopy.

Martin jumped on his board and started back. He peered to the side once more. Another flash of white drifted in and out of the trees, too large for a bird. Martin stopped, blood thumping loudly in his ears, his mouth dry. He spotted Pedro and Isabel waiting up ahead and hurried toward them.

"I just saw something over there," Martin yelled, pointing

to the trees, "something big and white."

Pedro's eyes flashed toward the woods. He spoke rapidly to Isabel.

Martin's skin got a funny crawly feeling. "What?"

"He says it's probably a bird, but we need to hurry. Pedro has to get home," Isabel answered, giving Martin a perplexed look.

What had seemed a long walk heading out to the secret path, took only five minutes on the return. Pedro promised to take them back another day.

Isabel and Martin arrived back in camp just in time for dinner. Martin turned to Isabel. "I really liked skating out there, but that place is weird."

"It's a little far away from things, but it's fine," she said, heading toward her tent to put her scooter away.

"But I know I saw something out there in the trees!" Martin insisted.

Isabel stopped and put a hand on one hip. "You were probably just nervous." Her voice sounded slightly impatient. "What could possibly be out there?"

Chapter 8

Family Secrets

As MARTIN WALKED to his tent that night, he heard arguing.

"I told you before we came you'd better not cause any trouble. So what do I hear from Mrs. Wells today?" Martin recognized the husky voice.

"I never wanted to come to this stupid place. You made me."

Martin peeked between trees. In the dark he could barely decipher the outline of Josh and his father about twenty feet away.

"That's too bad. You're here, and you better behave," Dr. Wilson hissed, leaning into Josh's face.

"I hate it." Josh's voice rang defiantly.

"Stop acting so immature. I think you like to embarrass your mother and me." He pushed Josh up against the tree and poked a finger in his shoulder. "I told you how critical this excavation is to my career. I can't afford to have you mess it up. But do you ever think of anyone except yourself? I've had it with you."

Martin couldn't imagine his dad doing that. He'd sit Martin down and talk quietly about taking responsibility for his actions and how he knew Martin was a good kid, but he'd slipped a little. Now Mom, on the other hand, she had a tendency to yell at him sometimes, but she would never push him around.

Dr. Wilson backed away. "I'd better not hear another word from Mrs. Wells, or you'll be sorry. I'll take away your Game Boy, and you'll be on detention."

Josh crossed his arms and turned away. "Like I care. There's nothing to do around this place, anyway."

"And another thing. Andy told me how you took his comic books this afternoon. Why can't you get along with your brother?" Dr. Wilson's voice rang with frustration.

"He's a royal pain, that's why. All you care about is Andy this and Andy that," Josh hissed back.

"You know we worry about his asthma. At least he listens to us."

"Oh, yeah—the little angel."

"Grow up, Josh. I have more important things to worry about. Now go to bed."

Martin ducked behind a tree as Dr. Wilson stomped off. Josh stood for a moment looking down before slamming his shoulder into the tree. He hunched over, and Martin heard muffled sobs. Josh could be a real jerk, but he felt kind of sorry for him. He knew the best thing was to slip away and not let Josh know he had overheard the conversation. He decided to go by his parents' tent and give them a hug good night.

Chapter 9

The Necklace

As THE WEEKS passed, life fell into a pattern around camp. Parents worked at the excavation site every day but Sunday. Mrs. Wells kept the kids busy and mostly happy with school. Josh got over his attitude and started participating.

The highlight of Martin's week was his twenty minutes on the computer when he could send e-mails home. At least he had contact with the real world.

Friday, October 13th

Hey Charlie,
Got your note. Too bad your parents won't let you fly here by yourself at Christmas. Maybe you could ask again later. They might change their minds.

Life around here is the same—totally boring. What I wouldn't give to see TV or a movie. I'm still hanging out with Isabel. She's okay. We go skating with our friend Pedro a couple of times a week. Josh has been nicer but he still won't do anything with us.

Isabel and I play soccer with the little kids sometimes after class. Josh's little brother Andy always asks me questions about skateboarding and reads my magazines over and over. They're getting pretty worn out.

Jenny spends all her time with Paolo, hanging all over him. But at least she's being nice to me.

Write soon. Hi to Ryan and Trevor.
Martin

*   *   *

One day after class, Martin returned to his tent to change his shirt. He had spilled a big splotch of bean sauce on it at lunch, and it was starting to smell funny. He found Josh reading the same book he had read ten times already, *Holes*. Josh always read or played his Game Boy, lying on his cot immobile.

"Hey, Josh," Martin said, trying to be friendly, although he wasn't sure why. "Isabel and I are going to the excavation site. Want to come?"

Josh eyed him suspiciously. "Maybe. Why are you going?"

"To look around. Dad said they marked some new quadrants off and started digging." Martin took off his shirt and threw it on the floor, reaching for a clean one in his plastic bin. "There's nothing else to do."

Josh sat up. "Okay. I guess so."

Isabel waited by the path. Her eyebrows rose slightly as she saw Josh. Martin had told her about the conversation he had overheard between Josh and his father. She felt sorry for Josh too, but he didn't make it easy.

Isabel smiled, "Hi."

"Hey," Josh mumbled, looking down at his feet.

They strolled across the meadow and turned down the road in the opposite direction from the village. It was a ten-minute walk to the excavation site. The road followed a curve in the stream to a flat area in the narrowest part of the valley. On the right side of the road, a series of outcroppings created narrow shelves up the mountainside.

Isabel pointed out two condors circling high in the sky, their massive wings creating shadows across the path. She stopped. "Look at that opening way up there in the rock. It must be a cave."

"Maybe we could explore in there," Martin said.

"How do you think you're going to get up there, genius?" Josh said.

"I guess it would be kind of hard." Martin shaded his eyes with his hand to see if there would be any way to climb up.

"Bet you can't throw a rock on that ledge," Josh challenged, indicating a shelf jutting out from the cliffs about twenty feet above them.

"Bet I can," Isabel responded immediately. She found a small rock and flung it hard. It bounced off the cliff below the ledge, falling back to the ground near Josh's feet.

"That was weak," Josh scoffed. He picked up a larger rock and threw it. It grazed the rim of the ledge and sailed back down, nearly hitting him on the head.

"Okay. Stand back. Now the master will show you how it's done," Martin said, as he picked up a heavy round rock with a great deal of fanfare. Isabel crossed her arms and rolled her eyes.

Martin took a few steps back and used his best pitching form, aiming for the back of the ledge. The rock hit hard, square against the cliff and bounced forward onto the ledge. Something fell and dangled over the side.

"Strike!" Martin yelled.

"What's that?" Isabel pointed.

"It looks like some kind of stone," Josh said.

Isabel surveyed the rocks. "Give me a foot up, and I'll get it."

"You'll never make it. It's shale. The rock will break away," Josh warned.

"I can do it." She sounded confident. "I've been rock climbing lots of times with my mother."

Isabel constantly surprised Martin. He didn't like to admit it, but she had more nerve than he did. She didn't seem to be afraid of anything. He wouldn't climb up there. No point in arguing, he knew when she got that determined look on her face, nothing could change her mind.

"This ought to be good," Josh said.

Martin sighed and clasped his hands together to form a step for Isabel's foot. Josh steadied her arm. She placed her free foot in a small crevice and grabbed two indentations in the rock, holding on precariously, her knuckles turning white. Somehow she propelled herself to another crack, then another and another. Clinging to the rock, she continued to climb, leaning into the cliff. Her right arm stretched its length to reach the hanging object, but stopped about six inches short. Her right foot scraped higher over the side, searching for a hold. As the left foot wobbled and started to slip, small pieces of rock gave way and rolled down. Martin cringed and sucked in his breath. Just in time, Isabel found a tiny outcrop for her right foot and quickly stepped up, grabbing onto the ledge for support.

"Told you!" she cried victoriously, peering down at Josh and Martin.

"Drop it to us," Josh suggested.

"It's stuck." Isabel tugged to work it free.

As she pulled it loose, Martin called, "Be careful coming—"

In an instant Isabel lost her balance and slipped. Martin watched paralyzed as she slid at least eight feet, hands wildly clutching at the rock.

Josh threw his arms out to Martin. "Hold on; we'll catch her!" As Isabel slid and then plummeted the rest of the way, the boys locked arms and maneuvered to break her fall. The three of them collapsed in a giant heap.

Josh sat up first, then Martin and Isabel, struggling to catch their breath. Wide-eyed and stunned, they checked arms and legs—nothing broken. Martin's elbow ached a little. Isabel's knees and hands were scraped and bleeding. She pulled a Kleenex from her pocket, spit on it and wiped gingerly.

Suddenly, a stream of small rocks cascaded down from the mountainside, forming a pile in front of them. Martin glanced up. "How did that happen?"

"It's probably an animal or bird." Josh stood up and brushed dirt off his shorts and t-shirt.

"Must be a really big bird." Martin continued to stare. Was that a shadow moving across the cave entrance?

Isabel dabbed at a scrape on her knee. "Thanks guys," she said with a touch of contrition. She whirled around and searched the ground.

"There it is." She picked up an oval, rust-colored stone, flat on one side and rounded on the other. A flower had been carved into the soft stone and a long piece of leather strung through a hole at one end.

"At least it didn't break," Martin said.

"It must be a necklace," said Isabel.

"Whatever it is, it's really old." Josh ran his fingers over the flower.

"But how did it get up there?" Martin questioned.

"Don't tell anyone we found it, or we won't have it long," Josh cautioned.

"You're right." Isabel placed it safely in her pocket. "We can keep it a secret for now. Just until we figure out where it came from."

Chapter 10

Inti, the Inca Sun God

"COME ON, LET'S go," Isabel said, once they had recovered from the fall. "My mother told me the wall Dr. Wells found is probably part of a house."

"I hope there's more going on today. Last week it was really boring," Martin said. "When did you see it last, Josh?"

"I haven't been there," he answered sharply. "I don't care about a bunch of dumb holes in the ground."

They walked in silence. Martin wanted to mention the book Josh had been reading but thought better of it.

At dinner the night before, Dr. Wells had reported that work was "progressing nicely." The excavation plan, methodically prepared over the first few weeks, had identified the possible layout of village walls and roads, along with the scale and topography.

As they approached the site, Martin saw strings running between metal stakes in the ground, marking a series of six-foot squares along the front of the exposed wall. Pete and Carey worked in the first two squares, carefully scraping away layers of dirt with hand-held hoes and brushes and placing what they removed into buckets. Samantha stood next to the quadrants, sifting the dirt through screens into a wheelbarrow. Two men

from the village hauled the discarded dirt to a disposal pile fifty feet away.

Pete looked up and waved.

Josh's mom and dad worked together in a third square. Dr. Lori Wilson appeared surprised. "Hi, Josh, I'm glad you came out to see the work."

"Where's your brother?" his dad demanded without offering a greeting.

"He's with Mrs. Bertolli." Mrs. Bertolli often returned to camp in the afternoons to entertain her twins and Andy, once school let out.

Dr. Henry Wilson frowned. "I told you to keep track of him."

Lori Wilson placed a hand on her husband's arm. "Henry, it's fine. Let Josh have some fun with Martin and Isabel." Josh stood next to Isabel, looking sullen.

Martin turned as Dr. Leonard emerged from a cluster of trees, winding around the rocks away from the site. He called out to Pete, "What have you found so far?"

"Not much. A lot of dirt." Pete wiped sweat from his forehead.

Dr. Leonard said, "Hey, kids. Glad you came to visit."

Martin's mom was talking with Dr. García and Dr. Wells in the tent, moving about highly animated. The tent had been set up as an office with a desk, chairs, file boxes, a table covered with the site plans, and another table for examining artifacts.

The examination table held a series of plastic bags filled with dirt and marked with the location and depth where the samples had been extracted.

Martin waited near the door.

"Hi, honey." Mom rushed over and planted a kiss on Martin's cheek. "Come see," she whispered, "but quietly. We haven't told the rest until we take a closer look." She nodded to the group working in the quadrants.

Martin had no idea what she meant, but he and Josh followed her across the path. Isabel trailed behind with Dr. Wells and Dr. García, as she tried to explain her scraped hands and knees.

"Carmen and Pablo worked this morning in the control pit, removing another layer of dirt," Mom started.

Josh looked puzzled. "What's a control pit?"

Martin wondered how Josh could have two archeologists for parents and not know. Apparently they didn't all talk together much about archeology or maybe about anything.

Mom glanced at Josh, surprised as well. "It's a test site, a place away from the excavation, where we don't think we'll find artifacts. We dig there first to understand the layers of earth and how to approach digging at the site. But we had quite a shock today."

They arrived at a pit about five feet square and six feet deep. Dr. Arturo knelt in the bottom, carefully brushing dirt off a raised gold object embedded in stone. He looked up smiling and rattled on in Spanish.

"Look at this!" Mom exclaimed.

"What do you think it is?" Martin asked.

Dr. Arturo stood and turned toward them, his face beaming. "It's definitely the Inca Sun god, Inti. We've done it. We've really done it! This is an Inca city."

Dr. Wells let out a deep protracted sigh and touched his hand to his heart. "This is all I have lived for—my dream." His voice sounded husky.

Martin winced, hoping Dr. Wells wasn't going to cry. He studied the half-uncovered object. It seemed familiar, with wavy lines fanning out, a mask in the center. He looked at Isabel, and she raised her eyebrows. Then he knew. It was the same mask from the plaza at the end of the secret path.

*   *   *

That evening Dr. Wells clinked his spoon and knife together, trying to quiet the dining hall. The team chatted, giddy with excitement.

"Everyone, if I could have your attention." He waited a few moments for the noise to quiet down. "I want to make a toast and say a few things about today's glorious discovery."

"Long live the Incas!" Mr. Bertolli called out, and everyone laughed.

Dr. Wells raised his paper cup, beaming. He had pulled out several bottles of wine to share for the special occasion. "Today is everything we hoped for. Here's to our great team and all the hard work ahead."

Martin's mom stood and raised her cup as she added, "And to you, Dr. Wells, for bringing our team here and making this a reality."

"Yes, Dr. Wells, we owe it all to you," Dr. Leonard added. A round of "cheers" and "here, here" filled the room.

Martin noticed Dr. Wilson's tepid toast as he squinted into a gloomy scowl. What was his problem? But he always looked unhappy.

Josh and Isabel sat across the table from Martin, clinking their cans of coke. Things at camp were turning out better than he expected. Josh even smiled at him.

"A few words of caution," Dr. Wells began again, his face serious. "We have a long way to go with this excavation, and hopefully we will find amazing treasures. It is essential that we keep the news of our discovery among ourselves for the time being. The more the outside world learns about our find, the greater the danger of looters arriving."

"I can tell you, many sites in Peru have been destroyed and treasures stolen," Dr. Arturo added, shaking his head slowly.

Martin watched Isabel's hand cover the pocket where she had put the necklace they found. A pang of guilt crossed over him. But they weren't going to keep it forever. Just for a while.

"It's a sad fact of life," Dr. Wells continued, "but for the safety of the site and our team, we must keep this secret. No e-mails to family or friends. Dr. Arturo and I will go to Lima in a few weeks to report to the ministry and hire a security force for the site." He stared around the tent. "But for now, we celebrate. Enjoy!"

Martin wished he could write Charlie about the find, but he sure didn't want to be the one giving away secrets. Other secrets already weighed on his mind.

Chapter 11

T'ika in Danger

"WHAT SHOULD WE tell Josh?" Isabel whispered to Martin. She had waited for him near the dining tent with her scooter over one shoulder. Pedro had come by early in the morning to suggest they visit the secret path that Friday afternoon. Two or three times a week, whenever Pedro could get away, they crept into the forest and rode along the smooth stones. But it had become more complicated since their tentative friendship with Josh.

"Do you think we should invite him?" Martin spun a wheel at one end of his skateboard. "He might feel left out if we don't."

"But I don't think Pedro wants anyone else to know about the path. He seems nervous enough about our being there."

As they spoke, Josh emerged from the tent. He eyed Isabel and Martin suspiciously. "What're you guys doing?"

"We're going riding. You could come if you want," Martin offered. Isabel reached behind his arm and pinched him hard. "I mean if you want to, but you probably have something to do."

"Where do you guys ride, anyway?" Josh took Martin's skateboard from him, gazing at it admiringly.

"There's a place over past the village. It's a twenty-minute walk," Isabel explained.

Martin knew Isabel was trying to discourage Josh. He wasn't big on walking or any other form of exercise. Occasionally they could get him into a soccer game, but it wasn't easy. His weight made him slow and awkward.

"It's too hot. I'm going to stay here and read." Josh handed the skateboard back. "I'm not supposed to leave Andy, anyway."

"Maybe we can play chess when I get back," Martin suggested.

Josh shrugged and headed for their tent.

As Martin and Isabel reached the path across the meadow, Andy appeared from out of nowhere.

"Martin. Can I come with you? I want to learn how to ride. Please, can I, please?" Andy tugged at Martin's t-shirt.

Martin laughed. "Not today, pal. But I'll show you soon. You'd better find Mrs. Bertolli or your brother."

Andy kicked the ground. "Okay. But promise?"

"Promise." Martin ruffled Andy's hair. Why couldn't he have gotten a little brother like Andy, instead of Jenny?

Pedro waited in the usual spot behind the trees. He seemed happy to see them as they hurried toward the path. Martin felt encouraged that he could say a few things to Pedro now that his Spanish was improving. But it was hopeless when Isabel and Pedro got going. They talked way too fast.

The air hung about them, heavy and damp in the hot afternoon Sun. Big fluffy clouds, tinged with gray, swirled across the sky. The rainy season had begun, and showers fell in sudden heavy bursts, creating streams of water that left the dirt road rutted and sticky.

"I hope it doesn't rain while we're riding," Martin said.

They reached the path and walked around to the back side of the cliffs. Pedro always gave the thumbs up when it was safe to ride. The three friends raced each other down the stones, laughing and calling out.

"Did you see that? I landed a kick flip!" Martin yelled. He had been teaching Pedro the names of various jumps.

When they stopped to rest, Pedro told them about the big festival in the village the next evening.

Martin strained to understand and said, "Repita, por favor," asking Pedro to repeat his words. Finally, he understood there would be music, dancing and lots of food.

"Cool," Martin responded.

"Cool," Pedro repeated, grinning.

Isabel and Pedro decided to trade their skateboard and scooter. Martin forged ahead while Isabel showed Pedro what to do. Rounding the final corner, he picked up his board at the square with the gold mask. Ever since that first day when he had seen a flash of white in the trees, this place made him jumpy. He walked to the center, his sneakers silent on the stones.

Birds squawked and something hooted in the canopy above. Martin turned toward the cliffs and listened to a muffled sound. It came from an outcrop of rock on the far side of the square. As he moved closer, the sound grew louder—or was it the thumping of his heart? He stepped slowly around the rock, his legs shaking slightly. Crouched against the cliff, a girl sat with her head in her hands and cried. Unlike the girls in the village with their blouses and multilayered skirts woven of brilliant hues, this girl wore a simple white dress, tied with a gold-colored sash around her waist. Sensing his presence, she looked up, startled. Fear passed into her eyes as she cowered farther into the cliff.

Martin took a deep breath. "Hola." He hoped she would understand he was friendly.

He heard Isabel and Pedro roll to a halt at the edge of the square. Martin stepped forward to wave to them as the girl cautiously stood up and peered out. She ran to Pedro and threw her arms around his neck. He looked confused but gently patted her back. They spoke to one another. Martin couldn't understand. It didn't sound like Spanish.

Isabel stood with her mouth open and leaned over to Martin. "They're speaking Quechua. Where did you find her?"

"Behind the rock. I heard her crying," he explained.

Pedro turned with a grim face and spoke, as Isabel translated, "I need your help in keeping another secret. This is T'ika. She's an Inca princess, and her life is in danger."

Chapter 12

The Lost City of Karu Orq'o

MARTIN AND ISABEL stared at one another, wide-eyed. Martin realized it must have been T'ika he had seen in the trees that first day.

Pedro asked them to sit down. He had a story to tell, and Isabel must translate. "I do not know where to begin. It is an ancient story, and you must promise never to tell anyone." Pedro looked at Isabel and Martin for reassurance. They both nodded solemnly.

"A very long time ago, the Incas came to this land and conquered the people living here. The Incas ruled over everyone until we became one people. The emperor ordered a great temple built at this site to worship Inti, the Sun god, much like Machu Picchu in the south. The new temple was the biggest and most sacred in the kingdom, and many Inca nobles and priests came here to live.

"Then the Spanish arrived in our country. They betrayed the Incas, killing Emperor Atahuallpa and his soldiers. Two of the emperor's wives and their children escaped to our village and were hidden in the temple. Other important nobles and priests came here as well, fleeing the destruction of the Spanish. They told how the Spanish killed many people, smashed the

Inca gods and stole the gold and silver."

As Martin listened, he thought of the stories Dr. Wells had told them in Cajamarca. But what did this have to do with T'ika? She sat quietly by Pedro's side, holding his hand, staring at Isabel and Martin with curious eyes.

Pedro continued, "To protect our temple and village, the priests devised a plan to trick the Spanish. They knew it would take time for the Spanish to find their way this far into the mountains, and by then the village would be ready.

"Part of the temple is built inside this mountain." Pedro pointed to the sheer granite cliffs. "Originally, two main entrances to the temple existed—one around the other side of the mountain, in a valley, and one where your parents are digging. There are also many secret entrances connecting to tunnels that lead into the temple. There is an entrance at this plaza.

"The priests knew the Spanish would travel to our valley by

the only road from Cajamarca, as you did. By the time they arrived, the villagers had covered the front side of the temple with dirt, layers and layers of dirt, basket by basket. They planted corn and beans up the side of the covered temple. The Spanish found Jalca and assumed it was nothing more than a simple village filled with peasants tending their crops, just as it appeared to your excavation team at first. Only now your group is close to finding the remains of the old temple entrance."

"That's why the square at the excavation site is buried so deep in the earth," Isabel murmured to Martin.

"And why all they've found is lots of dirt," Martin added. "But what about T'ika? What does it have to do with her?" He looked into her dark eyes filled with sorrow.

"As I explained, there is a valley on the other side of the mountain where the other entrance to the temple still exists. The Inca nobles, priests and many villagers moved to this valley and created a new city." Pedro leaned toward them, brushing his hair from his forehead. "This is called Karu Orq'o."

"Yes," Isabel said. "There was a Spaniard who wrote a letter about a hidden city named Karu Orq'o."

Pedro nodded. "A small band of Spaniards found their way here one year and discovered the temple. They were all killed except for one man. Somehow he escaped."

A chill rippled down Martin's back. What kind of secrets were they learning? It sounded dangerous.

Pedro continued, "For many years people feared the Spaniards would return. But the secret survived. At that time, over a thousand people lived in Karu Orq'o."

Isabel tilted her head sideways, frowning, "Can you still get to the city?"

"Yes. Through the secret tunnels." Pedro pointed up to the cliffs that ran the length of the valley. "The way T'ika came. The tunnels also lead to caves near the excavation site."

Martin thought of the cave high in the granite cliffs where they found the necklace. *Could they be connected?*

"But people don't live there now, do they?" Isabel asked, her voice incredulous.

Pedro's forehead formed a deep frown. "There are still about four hundred people living in Karu Orq'o. They are Incas, living as they have lived for hundreds and hundreds of years, following the same traditions, untouched by the outside world."

"But how . . . how could that happen? How could you keep such a secret all these years?" Isabel said.

"The Spanish who ruled our country were cruel and greedy." Pedro's voice turned harsh. "Our people hated them and vowed to protect the last Inca city. When Peru became independent from Spain, we still kept our secret, because a new set of invaders came to our land, creating again more danger."

"Who?" Martin asked.

"Archeologists," Isabel whispered, before Pedro could utter the word.

"Yes. And the looters who follow," Pedro added.

Chapter 13

Stolen Treasure

"SO T'IKA LIVES in Karu Orq'o?" Isabel said slowly. "But how did you meet?"

T'ika stirred at the sound of her name and spoke to Pedro in a timid voice. He seemed to reassure her that it was fine.

"About a year ago, T'ika and her younger brother Chatu were playing in a storeroom. They discovered a tunnel hidden behind jars of maize and covered with stones. They knew they were not supposed to go in, but the temptation was too great. When they followed the hidden passage through the mountain, they ended up here."

"I bet you were skateboarding," Martin chimed in.

"Yes. One day as I rested in the square, I saw them come from the rocks." Pedro stood and led them to the spot where Martin had found T'ika. He pointed to a small opening about four feet up behind a ledge that jutted out.

"Can I see?" Martin started to climb up, but Pedro stopped him.

"Not now. We must go back to the village. I must tell my father what has happened."

"What about T'ika?" Isabel asked.

"She will come with me." Pedro picked up his skateboard

and nodded his head to T'ika as he took her hand again.

"T'ika is such a pretty name," Isabel said.

Pedro looked at T'ika with tender eyes, "It means flower."

They walked up the stone path toward the village. T'ika clung to Pedro, her slender figure nearly as tall as his.

"Why is her life in danger?" Martin asked.

Pedro sighed. "Karu Orq'o is ruled by the descendants of Atahuallpa, always by a prince, in cooperation with the temple priests. T'ika's father ruled until two years ago when he died. Their mother died when Chatu was born. Chatu is only ten and cannot take over until he is sixteen. So T'ika's uncle, Prince Huzco, fills his place until then."

Pedro shook his head. "But there has been trouble lately in the temple, and Prince Huzco is suspicious of Chatu and T'ika. Perhaps Prince Huzco wants to remain as ruler and is trying to get rid of Chatu and T'ika. It is hard to know. This morning Prince Huzco took Chatu to his house and is holding him there. When T'ika found out, she hid and came to find me."

"What happened at the temple?" Isabel asked.

"Special offerings to Inti have been disappearing—

gold statues, cups and jewelry. Prince Huzco asked Chatu and
T'ika if they had taken them. He said perhaps they were planning
to run away, to betray their people. But even the necklace T'ika's
father gave her at her naming ceremony is missing. She had
placed it in the temple as an offering to Inti, asking for his help
with their problems. T'ika thinks someone knows she and Chatu
found the hidden passages and told Prince Huzco. Now she is
afraid of everyone."

"Maybe Prince Huzco is taking the things," Isabel guessed.

"Or it could be the priest, Shama," Pedro said. "Chatu and
T'ika used to play tricks on him when they were young, and he
never liked them. He may want to cause trouble."

Isabel looked up sharply. "What did T'ika's necklace
look like?"

Pedro consulted with T'ika before he spoke, "It is a special
red stone carved with a flower."

Martin met Isabel's wide green eyes. "I think we found her
necklace," he whispered.

Isabel explained to Pedro how they had found the necklace
on a ledge near the excavation site.

"The tunnels connect to the caves," Pedro said. "Whoever
took the necklace must have gone through the tunnels and
accidentally dropped the necklace from a cave above the
ledge."

"I saw something moving, but we thought it was an
animal," Martin said, remembering the pile of rocks that had
suddenly fallen around their feet.

"Then someone has found their way into the temple,"
Pedro said quietly. "Most likely a member of your excavation
team."

A drop of water fell on Martin's cheek, then more drops,
faster and faster. Engrossed in Pedro's stories, he had not
noticed the black clouds converging in the sky. A flash of

lightning crackled above, and a loud boom followed. Rain plummeted from the sky and flooded the path around them. Pedro herded them to cover under a palmetto tree's thick fronds. They crouched down, laughing at their wet hair and clothes. Even T'ika smiled and relaxed for a moment.

They waited for the storm to pass. Pedro assured them it would not last long. The rain rolled off leaves and formed puddles at their feet.

Martin happened to glance up as a man ran by on the path. He put his hand to his lips for everyone to be silent and crept forward to peek out. The man, his head covered with a blue jacket, loped along the slippery stones toward the square.

Martin turned back to his friends. "It's someone from our group," he whispered. "Maybe Dr. Wilson or Mr. Bertolli."

"Oh, no," Isabel said. "How did he find the path? What is he doing out here?"

Chapter 14

The Message

ISABEL AND MARTIN hurried back to camp to retrieve T'ika's necklace and deliver it to Pedro in the village. Martin felt relieved to be returning the precious necklace to its rightful owner.

"Do you think it was Dr. Wilson?" Isabel asked again as they scurried across the meadow toward camp.

"I keep telling you, all I could see were tan pants and a blue jacket. It was raining too hard," Martin repeated for the tenth time. Isabel wouldn't give up. She seemed kind of mad at him, like it was his fault he hadn't recognized the guy.

"I know is wasn't Dr. Wells or Dr. Arturo; he was too thin. And it wasn't my dad or Pete; the guy wasn't tall enough. Besides, I'd recognize my dad."

"Well, that leaves Dr. Wilson, Mr. Bertolli or Dr. Leonard," Isabel concluded. "Mr. Bertolli and Dr. Leonard are so nice." Her forehead wrinkled. "It must be Dr. Wilson. He's the only one who acts strange all the time."

"Do you think he could be taking the things from the temple?"

"He must be," Isabel said as she got a determined look in her eye, the look that made Martin uneasy. "We have to find out," she added.

"How? Tell our parents?" Martin said hopefully.

"Not yet. Let's see what happens. If someone is stealing the things from the temple, they're not going to tell anybody about the path or the plaza." Isabel stopped and put her hand on Martin's arm. "We promised Pedro we wouldn't tell."

"I know. I won't. But this is getting too scary." Martin's voice cracked slightly.

"What if it is Dr. Wilson? Poor Josh," Isabel whispered.

The team had already gathered for dinner. Isabel and Martin slipped into the dining tent, trying to be inconspicuous. Martin saw his mom cock her head toward him with an inquisitive look. Guilt weighed on his conscience. He had never kept secrets from his parents, certainly not life-and-death secrets.

Martin looked around. Everyone was there, including Dr. Wilson who wore jeans and a yellow t-shirt. Neither Dr. Leonard nor Mr. Bertolli had on tan pants, but with the rain this guy would have changed his clothes. He felt his own damp shorts and t-shirt sticking to him.

Would Dr. Wilson reveal the truth about the secret path and the square with the gold mask? He had a terrible feeling in the pit of his stomach. It meant trouble for the village and T'ika, possibly the ruin of Karu Orq'o. He didn't want to betray his friends, but maybe his parents could help. Why did Isabel have to be so insistent about keeping quiet?

Josh sat across from Martin and Isabel. "Where have you guys been? I looked all over for you."

"We got caught in the rain and had to hide in the trees. We were worried about the lightning," Isabel responded.

Martin was in awe of Isabel's ability to simply exclude certain details. It wasn't exactly lying. "Did you know the village is having a fiesta tomorrow night?" Martin tried as a diversion tactic.

"What—a bunch of dumb Mexican music," Josh said.

"Try Peruvian, whiz kid," Isabel responded. "It's going to be fun. I'm going."

"Yeah, well, whatever." Josh slouched in his seat looking put out.

"Tonight's my night on the Internet, but after I write some e-mails you guys want to play cards?" Martin offered, hoping to make peace. Isabel and Josh grudgingly agreed.

*   *   *

Martin sat at the computer in the communications tent, logging onto his family's e-mail site. Grandma had sent a note saying how much she would miss them on Thanksgiving. Charlie wrote that he and Ryan had been to a skate store in Chicago and met Tony Hawk. Charlie got his autograph.

But that paled in comparison to what he had learned today. He would have to keep his responses brief, since he couldn't tell them anything that was happening. They probably wouldn't believe it anyway. He wasn't sure he did.

As he pushed the send

button on his reply to Charlie, Dr. Wilson burst into the tent. Martin turned around, startled. A tiny shiver snaked up his back.

"What are you doing here?" Dr. Wilson asked gruffly.

"It's my—my family's night on the Internet."

Dr. Wilson shot a look at his watch and sighed impatiently. "I need to use the computer immediately. Give me five minutes, and you can have it back."

"I'm done, but Jenny's next." Martin saw the scowl on Dr. Wilson's face grow deeper. "But I'll tell her to wait until you're done."

Closing his connection, Martin headed for Isabel's tent. Josh walked toward him, eating a cookie.

"Ready for cards?" Josh asked.

"In a minute. I have to give Jenny a message. Why don't you go shuffle and deal?" Josh shrugged and sauntered off to the dining tent as Martin raced on to Isabel's tent.

"That was quick," Isabel said as Martin approached.

"Dr. Wilson came in all excited and wanted to use the computer." Martin looked around to see if anyone was near. "Do you think he's talked to Dr. Wells?"

"I don't know." Isabel came outside her tent. "Let's find out who he's writing."

"How are we going to do that?"

"Come on. We'll think of something." Isabel headed for the communications tent.

As they came around the corner, Jenny practically knocked them down. "Martin, why didn't you tell me you'd finished? I've been waiting for my turn."

"Dr. Wilson wanted to use it for a few minutes. I was coming to tell you," Martin said.

"Oh, honestly, everybody wants to use the computer tonight. It's not fair. It's our night. Well, come get me when it's free." Jenny stomped off.

Martin and Isabel carefully peered into the tent. Empty. "Look over there. Dr. Wilson and Dr. Leonard are talking." Martin nodded in the direction of the two men standing among the trees.

They tiptoed to the computer and leaned over to read the message on the screen.

> Miguel,
> Vamos el domingo. Nos encontramos mañana por la noche a las 9:00 en la plaza en Jalca para hablar de los detalles. Aparca el coche

"What does it say? Something about Sunday and tomorrow at the plaza?" Martin looked at Isabel, confused.

As Isabel started to explain, footsteps approached. "Quick. Get behind the file cabinet." Isabel pulled Martin's arm. They crouched low, barely squeezing into the tiny space, shoulders and legs touching. He thought he could hear her heart racing, or was it his own?

He closed his eyes and held his breath. Why did he let Isabel get him into these things? Someone sat at the computer and typed rapidly. Martin pried one eye open and leaned forward ever so slightly to look. But the desk was turned away from them, and the propane light on the desk blocked his view. All he could see were arms and fingers in motion. In a moment the chair rolled back, and the mystery writer disappeared.

After a few minutes, they slowly unfolded themselves from their hiding place and rushed to the computer screen, now devoid of clues. They walked out to find Josh talking with Dr. Leonard in front of the dining tent.

"Hey, guys, what took you so long?" Josh called.

"We're coming," Isabel said.

"So what did it say?" Martin whispered.

"He's meeting Miguel tomorrow night at the plaza to work out the details, and they leave on Sunday. Miguel has a car." Isabel looked at Martin. "They have to be stealing the things from the temple."

Martin's stomach felt sick. How could he face Josh as if everything were fine?

Chapter 15

The Festival

"**H**AVE YOU HEARD anything?" Isabel asked Martin as they wandered by the stream late Saturday afternoon. Bees sipped nectar from wildflowers and buzzed lazily around them.

"Nothing. I asked Dad if anything happened," he said shaking his head. "Dad would tell me." And he thought, *Dad would trust me to tell him something this important.* He didn't mention how close he had come to spilling the beans that morning. If his father hadn't been so preoccupied with work, rushing off to the site, he probably would have confessed.

"My mother didn't say anything either. She mentioned how odd it is that they haven't come to any substrata or rock at the site—only layers and layers of dirt."

Since the discovery of the Sun mask in the control pit, the pace of work at the excavation site had picked up. Martin's mom and Dr. García had been revising the excavation plan. Martin could hardly get his parents' attention these days.

"Obviously, Dr. Wilson isn't talking." Isabel frowned, pulling at the woven belt wound through the loops on her jeans. She had bought it from one of the women in the village who was said to be the best weaver in the region. The bright red background danced with a design of indigo blue llamas.

"Maybe he's planning on doing his own investigation and he sent the e-mail to that Miguel guy to help him," Martin suggested.

Isabel rolled her eyes, "Nice try. He has to be stealing the things from the temple," she said angrily.

He glanced distractedly at the bees. "You don't think these could be Argentine killer bees. We read about them last year in the *Science Newsletter*. They attack in swarms and kill you."

"Martin, don't be dumb," Isabel waved her hand at him impatiently. "We have to figure out what to do next."

"I feel so bad for Josh and Andy. This is terrible," Martin sighed.

"I know. But right now we need to find Pedro and tell him about the e-mail. We'll follow Dr. Wilson to his meeting with Miguel tonight."

Martin's chest tightened. "But how are we going to do that?"

"We'll follow him and find out what he's up to." Isabel turned. "I'm going to find Pedro."

* * *

Martin, Isabel and Josh departed early for the fiesta in the village. Despite Josh's protests, it hadn't taken much to persuade him to go. Martin didn't know why Isabel kept insisting that Josh come, as it only complicated things. They couldn't exactly tell Josh they were going to spy on his father.

As they headed across the meadow, Isabel asked in her sweetest voice, "Are your parents coming tonight, Josh?"

"Yeah. They're going to be celebrating, big time. My dad heard today he's getting tenure at the university." Josh straightened his t-shirt over his protruding stomach. "Hopefully he won't be so worried about everything now."

"What's tenure?" Martin asked.

"It's when the college makes a professor's position permanent," Isabel answered. "My dad has tenure."

"I guess they can't ever fire him now," Josh added. "My dad said coming on this excavation was a big plus in the university's decision."

Martin thought for a moment. "How did he find out?"

"They sent him an e-mail. He's been writing to the head of his department almost every day."

That explained why Dr. Wilson had been going to the communications tent constantly, but nothing else made any sense to Martin. Why would Dr. Wilson risk stealing Inca treasures, if he was about to get tenure? Behind Josh's back, Isabel shrugged and looked puzzled.

In the village, the street buzzed with activity. Wonderful smells wafted through the air from ovens where guinea pigs roasted and breads and sweets baked. Thick vegetable stews simmered slowly in pots. Despite his nervousness, Martin felt his stomach growl with hunger.

Children played in the street and followed after them down the road, singing and dancing with delight. They gobbled down little puffs of pastry dripping with sugar.

"Besitos," one of the little girls said, pointing to the sticky mess in her hand. *"¡Bueno!"*

"Bueno means good, but what's 'besitos'?" Martin asked.

Isabel laughed slightly, "It means little kisses."

As they came to the village square, Josh groaned, "Oh man,

that's disgusting. They're cooking a whole pig, head and everything." A wild boar, skewered on a thick spit, sizzled over an open fire.

"Don't look at it. It tastes just the same," Isabel said.

Martin could see Isabel's eyes darting about, seeking out Pedro. "There he is." Martin pointed to Pedro and several men arranging benches along the far side of the square. Another group of men tuned strange-looking instruments—an odd-shaped guitar, a long wooden flute, a shiny brass trumpet, a set of hollow wood tubes of different lengths tied together, called panpipes—like the ones they had heard played in Cajamarca.

Isabel waved, and Pedro met her in the square. They spoke as Pedro eyed the assembling crowd of villagers. Women brought more pots and large wooden bowls of food and placed them on tables near the roasting boar.

"Pedro has to help set things up for the dancing. He told me to watch for Dr. Wilson, and he'll join us soon," Isabel reported to Martin. Josh had wandered off to look at the food.

Martin glanced at his watch, 6:30 p.m. It could be a while. "Where's T'ika?"

"She's hiding in Pedro's house. They can't let anyone see her. Word might get back to her uncle."

"People in Jalca go to Karu Orq'o?" How did the two worlds mix?

"Pedro says the elders in the village know about Karu Orq'o. His father is one of them. They visit occasionally and pay tribute to the prince. The elders tell their children when they are grown." Isabel straightened her white skirt and blouse, tied at the waist with her llama belt.

"What did Pedro's father say about T'ika?"

"He's going to visit Prince Huzco tomorrow and try to clear things up for T'ika and her brother. But Dr. Wilson could make a mess of everything."

More villagers gathered in the square. The women smiled shyly in their layers of skirts made of bright colors and intricate patterns. They wore woven vests and hats in a variety of shapes with narrow to broad brims, each decorated with special ribbons or flowers. Men strutted before them in black pants and white shirts with woven vests or ponchos and knit caps like ski hats with earflaps. The hats looked kind of warm.

The Sun was slowly disappearing behind the brown barren peaks in the distance, leaving a haze of light in the sky. As the evening wore on, it would turn crisp and cold.

Everyone carried tall glasses of corn beer, chicha. The musicians drank, joked and got ready to play. Martin's parents and the other team members strolled into the square as the pig came off the spit. Dr. Wilson held his wife's hand, talking and laughing with Dr. Wells. The village men shook hands with Dr. Wells and the others, while women offered glasses of chicha.

The slow, haunting tones of the panpipes and flute drifted over the square as they feasted on boar and other delicious dishes. Martin grazed along the food tables, helping himself. Josh was on his second plate already. Isabel said she wasn't hungry.

After an hour, the music turned spirited, and couples began dancing traditional steps. Night enveloped the sky, free of the afternoon's threatening clouds. A dazzling array of stars twinkled above. The full Moon cast a golden light across the plaza, melting into the glow of candles wedged along windowsills.

The beat of pounding feet rumbled in Martin's ears. He checked his watch for the fiftieth time—9:13. No sign of Miguel yet. Where could he be? Drs. Henry and Lori Wilson danced with everyone else. How could Dr. Wilson act so normal, like nothing was happening? Wasn't he nervous? They waited, and 9:45 passed. The minutes crawled by until Martin thought he could hardly stand it.

Pedro danced with Isabel a few time, then circled the square, watchful. It was 10:42 when Pedro nodded ever so slightly to Martin and Isabel, indicating a man leaning against a house on the opposite side of the plaza. His face remained a shadow under a large cowboy hat. He didn't fit in.

Another man stepped in front of the mysterious stranger. Martin could only see his back through the throng of dancers. Who was it? The stranger struck a match and lit cigarettes for both men. Martin strained to get a glimpse, but someone danced by and stomped hard on his toes. He crumpled over in pain. When he looked again, the man was gone, and the stranger, presumably Miguel, stood alone, taking a deep drag on his cigarette.

Chapter 16

The Surprise

ISABEL PULLED MARTIN onto the plaza. "Dance with me!" she ordered.

"I don't know how," he yelled above the blaring trumpet.

What was she trying to do, anyway? He had never danced with a girl in his whole life, unless you counted his mom and grandma that time at his cousin's wedding. Martin and his friends had gone to the sixth grade graduation dance, but only Charlie and Trevor had gotten up the nerve to dance. Martin had been afraid of getting out on the dance floor and looking really stupid. He and Ryan had stayed on the sidelines, eating cookies and drinking Hawaiian Punch.

"Just move your feet," Isabel yelled. "Copy the others." She led him through the mass of wild dancers.

Martin stumbled and groped for her hand, afraid he might fall as dancers knocked into them. It looked to Martin like most people had polished off a few too many chichas, including his parents who spun by laughing. Isabel was tracking Dr. Wilson and moving in the direction of Miguel. Pedro stood close to Miguel, tipping his head slightly to Martin and Isabel.

In the blink of an eye, Miguel slipped behind the building where he had been standing. Martin thought of a magic show sleight of hand: Now you see it; now you don't. Dr. Wilson danced by, singing. *What an actor.* Martin whipped his head around as someone else disappeared behind a building in the corner of the plaza. Pedro took off after Miguel. Isabel yanked Martin's arm and headed to the spot where Miguel had stood.

She issued instructions, "I'll go first. Then you follow in a few seconds. Make sure no one sees you." She was gone.

Terror welled in his throat as he ducked behind the building. This was crazy. Isabel waited at the end of the house, peering out and holding her finger up for silence. The houses ran three-deep beyond the square. Martin could just make out two murky figures rounding the edge of a house on the third row down. He turned to Isabel. She stared back with the same astonished expression. It wasn't Dr. Wilson that Miguel had met. It was Dr. Leonard!

Isabel, Martin and Pedro crept across the tiny space toward the two men. The tip of Dr. Leonard's cigarette burned like a red beacon against the dark edge of the village. Low voices fired back and forth, quickly rising and falling, barely audible. The words hung in the air, undecipherable. They spoke in Spanish. All this danger, and Martin could still only pick up a word here and there, even though he was getting used to the language. Just his luck! At least Isabel and Pedro understood.

"Hey, what are you guys doing back here?" A loud voice rang out from behind them.

Dr. Leonard dropped his cigarette and crushed it with his foot all in one movement. He and Miguel stood very still.

Martin's heart stopped as he swung around to find Josh standing across the way, the lights of the plaza outlining his broad silhouette.

"We thought we saw Andy and the twins come out here," Isabel sang out, sauntering toward Josh. "We were worried they might get into trouble."

Martin marveled at her quick response. How did she think of these things?

"My parents just took Andy back to camp. It's way late for him. I think I'll go back, too. I'm tired."

"Good idea. Wait for us." Martin headed for the square, taking giant strides, but stopping short of running.

*   *   *

"I can't believe Dr. Leonard is the one." Martin shook his head. "Of course, I'm glad it's not Josh's dad."

"We were wrong, I guess." Isabel looked around cautiously. They were alone at the breakfast table, except for Mrs. Bertolli and the twins at the other end. Everyone else slept in after the late night.

"It all makes sense now," he went on excitedly. "Do you remember the day we found the necklace? I thought I saw someone in the cave."

Isabel looked unsure, "Yeah?"

"Then at the excavation site, Dr. Leonard came around the hillside, all sweaty and out of breath. He must have come from the tunnels. He probably dropped the necklace by mistake."

"Hmm, maybe. But what about the e-mail to Miguel?"

"I couldn't see who was writing. And Dr. Leonard was standing there with Josh when we came out." He leaned forward. "What did they say last night?" Isabel had not been able to tell him about the conversation the night before with Josh around.

"Dr. Leonard's meeting Miguel at noon today somewhere in the forest, and they're driving to Cajamarca," she whispered. "Miguel has a Land Rover waiting part way up the road."

Martin rolled his churro in a pool of cinnamon sugar on his plate. Churros were his favorite. "What do you think they're doing?"

Isabel gave him one of her exasperated looks. "Obviously they've taken the things from the temple, and they're leaving with them."

"We have to tell our parents and Dr. Wells," Martin said with growing alarm.

"Not yet, please. Pedro wants to give his father a chance to visit Prince Huzco today. We're meeting them in ten minutes. They want to leave while everyone is in church."

Martin opened his eyes wide. "We're going to Karu Orq'o?"

"No. We're going along to guard the entrance at the plaza," Isabel answered, as if she were suggesting a swim at the beach.

Martin gulped. "Guard the entrance? From who?"

"Oh, for heaven's sakes, I just mean we'll keep an eye out for anything different. Take your skateboard and meet me in five minutes." She took a last sip of her cocoa. Glancing over her shoulder as she walked out, she added, "Don't look so worried. Nothing's going to happen."

Chapter 17

Standing Guard

MARTIN LEFT JOSH snoring loudly in their tent and met Isabel with his skateboard. As they started to leave, his mom and dad walked gingerly toward the dining hall. Mom massaged her forehead as if it hurt.

"Hi, Martin," Dad said softly. "You're up early."

"It's eleven, Dad." Martin raised his eyebrows to Isabel. "We're going riding."

"Have fun and be careful." Mom gave him a peck on the cheek. "You have your helmet, I see."

"Where exactly do you two ride?" Dad asked. "I've never been able to picture the spot."

"Umm, I, I told you—" Maybe Dad knew something was going on.

"It's past the fields behind some trees; a place Pedro showed us," Isabel explained airily. "Could you tell my mom we'll be back in a while?"

They took off before Martin's parents could ask anymore questions. Andy stood by a tree, kicking a soccer ball and looking bored. He waved to them with that envious face he got every time Martin departed with his skateboard.

Pedro and his father Juan waited in the usual spot. Juan

nodded grimly and led the way, appearing deep in thought. Martin didn't know much about Prince Huzco, but he was glad he didn't have to face him.

As they walked silently through the trees, Martin's head swam with questions. Was it really possible that Dr. Leonard had found the tunnels and stolen things from the temple? Was Juan going to tell Prince Huzco about Dr. Leonard? Did the prince know about the excavation? Once the excavation team uncovered the old entrance to the temple, wouldn't they discover the truth anyway? Surely it wouldn't be long before the world learned about Karu Orq'o. It was all too confusing and complicated. He wished he had talked to his dad. As soon as they got back to camp, he would go directly and tell him the whole story, whether Isabel agreed or not.

They followed the stone path to the point where they normally began riding. Isabel and Martin looked uncertainly at Pedro. Did Juan approve of Pedro and his friends riding on the path? Pedro asked if they could skate.

"Sí," Juan smiled broadly at Pedro.

They took off, enjoying the speed and freedom, the release from the troubling events consuming their lives. They waited at the plaza for Juan to catch up.

"My father is taking me with him to meet Prince Huzco," Pedro announced. "It is time to introduce me." He looked down shyly. "I am going to ask his permission to marry T'ika."

To his amazement, Martin had caught most of what Pedro had said. He looked at Isabel. "Did he say 'marry T'ika'?"

Isabel nodded.

Martin contemplated the news. "But aren't they kind of young?"

Isabel translated.

"We will marry in two years when T'ika is sixteen," Pedro explained. "I will ask her uncle if she can come to live in my village."

Martin stared at Isabel. Marriage was for adults, people in their twenties and older. He tried to imagine Jenny getting married. What a scary thought! But life in Jalco moved at a different pace.

Juan arrived at the plaza and checked once more on T'ika's necklace nestled in his shirt pocket. He would show Prince Huzco and explain its discovery as proof that someone from outside had been stealing the things from the temple—not Chatu and T'ika. Juan and Pedro ascended to the opening in the rocks. Pedro waved goodbye, looking hopeful and nervous.

Isabel and Martin waited at the plaza. Martin still wasn't sure what they were supposed to do, but he settled down against the rocks next to Isabel. Martin leaned back against the stone. The warm Sun and melodic buzz of insects made his eyes feel droopy. It had been a late night.

Suddenly he felt someone nudging his arm. He had trouble opening his eyes.

"Martin, someone's coming!" Urgency filled Isabel's voice. "Scoot over here behind the rocks."

Martin scrunched up against Isabel, drawing his knees to his chest. He heard voices speaking in Spanish. Peering through a crevice, he spied Dr. Leonard and Miguel walking rapidly across the square, carrying shovels.

He watched until he had to lean out around the rocks to keep them in view. They walked into the trees on the far side of the plaza and began digging.

"They must be digging up the things he stole from the temple," she whispered.

His heart raced. "We've got to get out of here and tell our parents."

She nodded solemnly. "You're right. If we're really quiet, they probably won't see us. Stay close to the cliff."

As they started to edge out, a faint call drifted across the plaza. "Martin. Hey, Martin. Where are you?" The voice grew nearer, tentative and tiny. "Isabel. Martin. I want to skateboard with you."

Martin froze. Isabel pulled him back behind the rocks. Peeking through the crevice again, he saw Andy shuffle into the square.

Dr. Leonard ran into the plaza. "What are you doing here, Andy? How did you find this place?"

"I'm looking for Martin and Isabel. I followed them from camp, but then I couldn't see them anymore, and I found this path and I—" Andy's voice became wobbly. "I think maybe I'm lost." A little sob escaped as Andy stared up at Dr. Leonard.

"It's okay. You can come

with me," Dr. Leonard said, his voice calm. Miguel came to the edge of the trees with his shovel.

Andy spotted the man and started to back away. "No. I'm going back. I can find the camp."

Dr. Leonard lurched forward and grabbed Andy's arm. "No. You'll stay here. I don't want you to get lost, Andy," he murmured reassuringly. "My friend and I are just playing a game. We're pretending we have a buried treasure. You can play too. It will be our secret."

Isabel squeezed Martin's arm and sucked in her breath. Martin felt sick to his stomach with fear. Things had gone too far, and he had kept too many secrets. If anything happened to Andy, it would be his fault.

Andy gazed wide-eyed at Miguel and began crying out loudly, "I want my mom and dad! I want to go back right now!"

"Stop crying!" Dr. Leonard barked, dragging Andy toward the woods. "I'm going to have to tie you up and put a gag in that loud little mouth."

Chapter 18

The Rescue

MARTIN TORE FROM Isabel's grip and headed for Andy and Dr. Leonard. He had to save him. But someone else raced toward them. *Josh!* Unsure what to do, Martin retreated behind the rocks again, unnoticed.

"Let go of my brother!" Josh shouted, running at full speed. "What do you think you're doing?"

Dr. Leonard looked up startled and let go of Andy's arm. Andy ran to Josh and hid behind him.

Josh stood a few yards away, panting, "What're you doing out here, anyway?" He stared at the Sun mask. "What is this place?"

Martin bit his lip as he caught a glimpse of Miguel quietly dropping his shovel and moving stealthily toward the brothers. Then Josh caught site of him as well. "Run, Andy, run!" Josh cried, spinning around, clutching Andy's hand and scrambling toward the path.

Miguel started after them, but Dr. Leonard yelled in Spanish, "No! Let them go. I don't want anyone hurt. We have to get out of here." He continued to bark orders at Miguel. He stopped for a moment and gazed around the square. His eyes narrowed as he locked onto the rocks where Isabel and Martin hid.

Isabel squeezed Martin's hand with cold, shaking fingers. They both held their breath and watched through the crevice as Dr. Leonard stood a moment longer and then returned to digging with Miguel. Isabel and Martin crouched motionless for several minutes, but they knew it was now or never. Martin nodded to her and stood up, clutching his skateboard and helmet to his stomach. They edged along the cliff toward the path. His heart pounded, and his legs felt weak. As they reached the corner of the square and slipped behind a tree, they looked back.

The two men, dragging a large duffel bag out of the ground, had not seen them. The bag appeared bulky and heavy. Dr. Leonard looked around the square again, as if he sensed a presence. The men headed toward the tunnel opening as they struggled with the bag. They reached the rocks where only moments before Isabel and Martin had hidden, below the opening.

Isabel and Martin slipped from tree to tree and waited until they were well away from the square, to break into a run. Finally they hopped on their skateboard and scooter, gliding over the stone path at top speed, desperate to get back in time.

As they neared the end of the path, Josh and Andy came into view, turning and waving wildly.

"Did you guys see Dr. Leonard down there?" Josh's voice rang out high and squeaky. He was sweating profusely and gasping for breath. Andy still held his hand and cried softly.

"Yeah. We saw everything that happened," Martin said quickly. "It's a long story, but we have to get back to camp right away and tell our parents and Dr. Wells what's going on."

Josh strained his neck, looking down the path. "Are they coming after us?"

"No. It's okay. Just follow us out and get back to camp," Isabel said.

Once they had made it through the curtain of leaves, Isabel and Martin ran ahead of Josh and Andy. They raced to the road, past the village and across the meadow. Martin's lungs burned, and his sides ached.

As they approached camp, Martin started screaming, "Mom, Dad, help! Mom! Dad!" His parents sprang up from where they were reading under a tree. Isabel's mother, Dr. and Mrs. Wells and the Wilsons ran out.

Isabel in Spanish and Martin in English began telling their tale.

"Whoa, hold on," Martin's dad said. "Is anyone hurt?"

"No," Martin shook his head. "But we have to stop them quick."

"Have you seen Andy or Josh?" Dr. Lori Wilson broke in, worried. "I haven't been able to find either of them."

"Andy's with Josh. Josh saved his life," Martin said. Dr. Henry Wilson stared with his mouth open.

"Slow down and explain. What's all this about?" Dad put his arm around Martin's shoulder and held him. Martin realized he was shaking violently.

"Dr. Leonard is stealing these Inca treasures from the temple. Dr. Wells, there's a temple, and the excavation site is only— well anyway, there's this really bad guy with him, and they're going to get away if we don't hurry!" Martin blurted out.

Meanwhile Isabel had been explaining to her mother, in a more concise and logical order, the events that had taken place. Dr. García relayed the story, as Martin and Isabel filled in the details. Josh and Andy arrived in time to tell their part of the tale.

Dr. Wilson put his hand on Josh's shoulder. "Son, I'm so proud of you. That was very brave."

Dr. Wells had been listening, his mouth agape. "I can't believe it. I can't believe any of it. Not Jim!"

"It's true. We have to stop him now. We don't have time to waste talking!" Isabel cried.

"Yes, of course," Dr. Wells sighed and shook his head. He stood up straight and recovered his director's voice, "Carmen, you go to the village. Find José from the crew and have him gather a group of men."

"Harvey and I will find the rest of our group," Martin's mom volunteered.

"We'll send a group back to this secret plaza. Someone in the village will know how to get there. Right Isabel?" Dr. Wells asked.

She nodded.

"The rest of us will wait by the excavation site for them to come out of the tunnels," he continued. "I want the children and women to stay at the camp."

"Wha . . . what?" Isabel stammered. Her mother spoke sharply, and Isabel frowned.

Martin felt relieved. All he wanted was to sit down. His mother hugged him close and left with his father. "I'll be right back," she said.

Dr. Wells looked around. "Dr. Wilson, you had best bring along some rope. We may have to tie them up."

Chapter 19

Capturing Thieves

EVERYONE SPRANG INTO action to alert the village and other team members. Isabel, Martin and Josh settled in the dining hall with the twins and Andy. Mrs. Wells brought sodas and cookies for the group. Dr. Lori Wilson cradled a still-frightened and sniffling Andy in her lap as Isabel and Martin told Josh the whole story.

"Why didn't you guys tell me about this before?" Josh said, staring at them with accusing eyes.

"We promised Pedro not to tell," Isabel replied.

"I wanted to tell you and my parents, too." Martin took a bite of his chocolate chip cookie, thinking of the nagging guilt he had felt for weeks. He felt even guiltier that they had suspected Josh's dad of taking the things from the temple. He and Isabel hadn't mentioned that part of the story to anyone.

"How did you find the secret path?" Isabel asked.

"I saw Andy leaving camp by himself, and I went after him, but he ran too fast. I couldn't catch up with him until we got to the plaza."

"You were very brave." Isabel looked at Josh with admiration.

Josh turned slightly pink. "Andy's kind of a pain, but I guess I wouldn't want to lose him."

Andy stood up and came over to hug Josh. "Thanks for saving me." Dr. Wilson wiped her eyes as Mrs. Wells patted her on the shoulder.

Martin's mom returned with the other women and Jenny. Paolo had gone with the men. They waited nervously. The minutes crawled by.

"Let's play gin rummy," Martin said, desperate for something to ease the tension.

"I wonder what's going to happen now that the secret of Karu Orq'o is out?" Isabel shuffled the cards and began dealing. Her hands still shook slightly.

Josh fanned his cards out. "Dr. Arturo and Dr. Wells will have to report to the government in Lima."

"I feel bad that we had to tell, but we couldn't help it, of course," Isabel said.

Martin looked pointedly at Isabel. "We should have told our parents sooner. I mean, eventually the excavation would have uncovered the entrance to the temple and the tunnels, anyway. They were going to find out."

"You're right," Isabel sighed. "I don't know how Juan and the others thought they could keep this secret. I wonder how the visit is going with Prince Huzco."

"At least now we can prove who took the things. We'll have to tell them right away." Martin put three sixes together in his hand.

"This means the end of the excavation," Josh said.

Martin looked up, startled, "You think so?"

"Yeah. How can you excavate an existing temple and city with people living there?"

Jenny shot to attention. "I'm not going home," she responded in that familiar, defiant voice Martin hadn't heard since they'd arrived at camp.

He considered the possibility of leaving. He felt confused.

It was all he had wanted when they'd first arrived, but now it didn't sound as appealing. Peru had turned out to be the most exciting experience of his life. What about Isabel, Josh and Pedro?

"We could stay to uncover the front side of the temple," Isabel speculated.

Martin walked over to the door and peered out. "Where are they? Do you think they've caught them yet?"

"I can't stand the waiting," Isabel said.

Martin sat down to take his turn as shouting reached their ears.

Martin, Isabel and Josh were the first ones out the door. The commotion came from the direction of the village. Dr. Leonard and Miguel were racing across the meadow, headed for the stream. About a hundred feet back, a group of men from the village chased after them.

"Come on," Isabel yelled, taking off.

Before anyone could stop them, Martin and Josh chased after her. She led them straight into the path of the fugitives.

Martin could hear their mothers frantically calling to them. His legs were tired, and he stumbled over a mound of dirt and fell. He stood up again as Dr. Leonard and Miguel approached. Both men were looking backwards, unaware of anything but the men pursuing them.

"Trip them!" Isabel screamed.

Martin and Josh dove in front of the two men, catching them by surprise. The men fell to the ground with a great thud. Isabel jumped on top of Dr. Leonard's legs before he could get up, and Martin held onto an arm. Out of the corner of his eye, Martin watched Miguel roll over and stand, but Josh grabbed his leg and held him back. He tried to kick Josh off but lost his balance and fell again. Their mothers held the two men down, latching onto flailing arms and legs. A jumble of people surrounded them. In a few seconds, the men from the village had arrived with Dr. Wells, Martin's dad and the others close on their heels.

They tied the two men to chairs in the communications tent, as a relieved and shaken group crowded round.

Martin's father began, "When we arrived at the excavation site, we saw Dr. Leonard and this man coming through the trees, carrying a bag. The minute they saw us, they turned and ran in the other direction. It took us a while to find the entrance to the tunnel. It was hidden in the cliff."

"Harvey went in after them," Dr. Wilson continued, "and found the bag stashed in a side tunnel. I guess they realized they couldn't carry it and hope to get away." He scowled at the two men.

"We weren't sure how many openings they could escape through," Dad went on excitedly. "I kept after them. What an incredible set of tunnels!"

"Fortunately, they went back to the plaza where you left them," said Dr. Wilson, turning to Martin, Isabel and Josh.

"I just come with the crew," Mr. Bertolli broke in, "and we wait in the square, and is movement in the trees." He waved his hands wildly, "We start to run after them!"

"Oh, you all think you're such big heroes, don't you," Dr. Leonard spat out the words from his chair.

Dr. Wells sank into a chair next to him, his face sad. "Jim, I can't believe you would do this. After all the years we've worked together. I've treated you like my own son. Why?"

Dr. Leonard stared back sullenly, "I'm always in your shadow. I never get credit for doing anything—*your* expedition, *your* team," he said angrily.

Dr. Wells shook his head, "I never knew you felt that way. You should have told me. But how did you know about the temple?"

"I didn't for sure. I read the Spanish documents and decided to do a little exploring on my own. I happened upon the entrance near the site." He smiled. "I'm more resourceful than most." He paused a moment. "I wasn't doing it for money. I wanted credit for finding the temple. When I discovered people living there, I didn't know what to do."

"Now what?" Dr. García asked.

"I suggest we take two cars and deliver these men to the police in Cajamarca," Dr. Arturo spoke up. "It's a matter for the authorities. The crew from the village can help us."

Dr. Wells put his hand on Dr. Leonard's arm. "Jim, I'll call the American Embassy. I'll try to help you straighten this out."

"Harvey could go with you, Pablo," Martin's mom suggested. "You look awfully tired, Richard."

"Perhaps. This is more excitement than I ever imagined," Dr. Wells agreed. "Pablo, you can call Lima and arrange a conference with the Ministry next week."

"Right," Dr. Arturo nodded. "In the meantime, you can gather more information about the city of Karu Orq'o."

"Remarkable. It's simply remarkable," Dr. Wells murmured. "Beyond imagination!"

Dad put an arm around Martin. "You should have told us about this, Son."

"I'm sorry. It's just that we promised Pedro, and I didn't know what to do. But I guess sometimes you have to tell secrets when people might get hurt."

"I think you've learned an important lesson," Dad hugged him close.

Dr. Arturo carefully opened the duffle bag, pulled out a gold cup and smiled. "We'll need to return the stolen property to its proper owners."

Dr. Wells gawked. "How lovely it is." Then in Spanish he asked José if he could meet with the village leaders about contacting Prince Huzco.

"We will hold a council meeting as soon as Pedro and Juan have returned," José responded. He added sadly, "Everything will be different now."

"Yes," Dr. Arturo agreed. "We must guard our secret as long as possible. If we are not careful, this place will be crawling with reporters." He looked at Dr. Leonard, "And most certainly more looters."

Chapter 20

Prince Huzco

MARTIN EXAMINED HIS wardrobe and wondered if it was okay to meet a prince in a t-shirt and shorts. Maybe his Hawaiian print sports shirt would be better.

"Come on, Martin. It's time," Mom called outside the tent.

He emerged to find her waiting with that smile she got whenever he did something right.

"I'm so proud of you, darling." She kissed him on the cheek and hugged him. "Josh and Isabel are waiting up by the path with Dr. Wells."

Dad put a hand on his shoulder. "Remember to be respectful and follow the directions of Juan and José."

Mom straightened his shirt collar. He gave them a smile and headed toward the path. This had to be the weirdest and most exciting thing to ever happen in his life—visiting a real live Inca city and meeting a prince.

Dr. Arturo and Martin's dad had delivered Dr. Leonard and Miguel to the police in Cajamarca. They had returned the night before. The minister of the interior of Peru would arrive the following week to meet Prince Huzco and work out arrangements to protect Karu Orq'o. Dr. Wells held hopes of heading a team along with Dr. Arturo to study and document

Inca life there. Juan, José and several Jalca elders had spent the last two days reporting on the captured criminals and preparing Prince Huzco and the people of Karu Orq'o for the coming changes.

The prince had been interested in the three young people who helped solve the mystery of the temple's disappearing treasures. He wanted to meet them personally and thank them. It seemed a fitting introduction to the outside world. After much discussion, it was decided that only Dr. Wells would accompany them. They did not want to overwhelm Prince Huzco and his people with outsiders. Martin knew how hard it must be for his parents to stay behind, but hopefully they would have their chance soon.

"Come on. We don't want to be late," Isabel called, as Josh grinned and raised his eyebrows.

Dr. Wells looked anxious to lead the way along the well-worn path to the village. At dinner the night before, he could hardly contain himself; he was so excited about their visit.

José and Juan waited in the village plaza. T'ika stepped out of Pedro's house, holding his hand, and they joined the group.

"Is T'ika going home?" Isabel asked Pedro.

"For now," he said, squeezing her hand, "but I can go to visit every Sunday. Prince Huzco says she can come to Jalca for special holidays."

"And Chatu?" Martin asked in Spanish.

"Prince Huzco wants Chatu to spend time in Jalca," Juan explained, speaking slowly for Martin and Josh to understand. "He may go to school with Pedro and learn Spanish. Chatu will share a special role with his uncle in ruling Karu Orq'o until he is old enough to take over."

José nodded as the group headed down the road toward the stone path. "Prince Huzco is a wise man to realize Chatu must be prepared for the outside world."

"Indeed," said Dr. Wells. "I admire Prince Huzco. It's not every man who could admit he was wrong in accusing T'ika and Chatu of stealing the treasures."

"Lucky for you, Pedro. It was a good time to ask him about marrying T'ika," Josh laughed. Pedro nodded with a sly smile.

"In two years we'll come back for the wedding," Isabel said.

"Yes," Pedro said. "We will have a big celebration, and you must be here."

Isabel shook her head. "I still can't believe we're going to meet a prince and—well, any of it." She turned to Martin and Josh and asked in English, "Are you nervous?"

"Nah. Why would I be nervous?" Martin laughed. "Maybe a little."

"Yeah, me too," Josh admitted. "Hey, Dr. Wells, do we have to wear a burden on our back and not look Prince Huzco in the eyes to show respect?"

"Very good, Josh. I see you've been reading up on the ancient Inca traditions," Dr. Wells responded. Isabel, Martin and Josh had poured over every book on the Incas they could find in camp for their visit. "But that only applied to the emperors.

Juan tells me that with Prince Huzco we simply need to bow slightly when introduced and only speak when he speaks to us."

Martin thought that should be pretty simple, given his knowledge of the Quechua language.

"José says they have a special celebration planned for us," Dr. Wells continued.

Martin looked up, alarmed. "I hope they aren't going to sacrifice a llama or anything while we're there."

Isabel's face filled with horror as she looked nervously at T'ika. "They don't still sacrifice young girls, do they? I don't think I could bear talking to them if they do."

Dr. Wells smiled. "No, dear. They've made a few concessions to the modern world and given up that practice. They do occasionally offer animals to the gods, but I don't think we'll see that today." Dr. Wells had spent the previous day with José and Juan, asking an endless stream of questions.

They reached the cave entrance and one by one climbed to the narrow slit into the tunnel. Dr. Wells had to be assisted by Juan and Pedro to heft his large frame as he huffed and puffed.

"It's no fun getting older, children, let me tell you!" he laughed good-naturedly.

Once inside the rocks, the low, dark tunnel twisted around for ten feet before suddenly opening up. Dr. Wells and José turned flashlights down the dark space.

"I'm glad we can stand up," Martin murmured. He ran his fingers over the worn and remarkably smooth rock.

"Hope no one's claustrophobic." Josh's words echoed off the walls.

"Are there any spiders in here?" Isabel asked in a low voice.

"No. Just bats," Josh offered as he ran his fingers along Isabel's neck. She screamed and hit his arm.

"All right, children. We don't have far to go," Dr. Wells assured them, looking with interest at symbols etched into the rock wall.

They continued down the tunnel for ten minutes and crossed at least a dozen side tunnels. In the confined space their footsteps reverberated like the clip clop of horses' hooves. The stale air felt close around Martin, and his stomach began to churn. The tunnel narrowed, and the ceiling became low again. They were forced to crouch down on hands and knees. Crawling the last few feet, they emerged into a small, dimly lit room where a large urn had been pushed aside from the opening. Baskets lined the walls, stacked three high and filled with dried corn and grain.

Isabel peered into the baskets. "Where are we?" she asked in Spanish.

"It's the storage room where T'ika and Chatu found the tunnel," Pedro said. "This way." He led them through a door into a larger room filled with more baskets overflowing with red beans and potatoes. Sunshine poured through an arched doorway.

They stepped out into daylight and squinted against the bright rays. Three men waited. Two carried spears decorated with red and yellow feathers. Their pointed metal helmets, surrounded by a band of the same feathers, danced with sunlight. The third man wore an impressive-looking headdress woven from fabric and gold with blue feathers. He nodded and greeted Juan and José. Martin knew his mouth was hanging open. All he could think was these guys looked like they were off a movie set.

Juan turned to the group, "This is one of the priests, Lantic. He will take us to the plaza where the prince waits for us."

"Why are these guys wearing dresses?" Martin whispered to Josh. Their loose white outfits, decorated across the hem with colored patterns, hit just above the knees. Strings of red feathers were tied around their calves. Long dark hair fell down their shoulders, and gold circles hung from their ears. The priest wore a huge gold circle tied with a leather string around his neck.

Josh made a face. "They're not dresses. They're tunics. Like the Greeks and Romans wore."

Martin shrugged. "Oh. They look a lot like dresses to me."

"Nice knees, huh?" Isabel said under her breath, giggling with Martin. Dr. Wells frowned at them.

The men led them down a set of stairs to a narrow street. Stone houses with thatched roofs reached several stories high. They traveled along a maze of streets until they reached a huge open plaza. The visitors stopped and stared.

Dr. Wells took a deep breath. "Oh, my goodness, I had no idea."

The people of Karu Orq'o filled the edges of the stone plaza, waiting for the strange foreigners to pass their way. A few children smiled and others hid their faces behind their mothers' skirts. Women wore tunics like the men, only long to their ankles and tied around the waist with colorfully patterned sashes.

Isabel nudged Martin and nodded toward the gold Inti mask embedded in the center of the plaza. It was like the other two at the secret plaza and the excavation site, only twice as large.

Martin's voice filled with awe. "Wow! Look at that throne." At the far end of the plaza stood a huge stone structure formed of a series of giant blocks in a pyramid shape. A set of stairs ran down the front. An older man and a young boy sat on stone chairs at the top.

T'ika waved excitedly.

"I'd have to guess that guy's Prince Huzco," Josh quipped.

"If he wanted to impress us, I think he's been quite successful," Dr. Wells added.

Lantic bowed his head and urged them to step forward toward the prince. Martin felt his mouth go dry. "What would he say to a prince?"

Chapter 21

The Celebration

LANTIC LED THEM across the plaza as people nodded their heads in greeting. He stopped in front of the throne, bowed to Prince Huzco and Chatu and then to the guests. Chatu's face beamed with excitement, and he squirmed in his seat as if barely able to hold himself back from running down the stairs.

Prince Huzco and Chatu rose from their seats, dressed in fine tunics and headdresses woven in intricate designs of gold garnished with magenta and turquoise feathers. Prince Huzco, an imposing figure, peered down.

Martin glanced around uneasily. Fierce-looking guards stood at attention on either side of the steps. He wondered if these people still carried a grudge against the Spanish. And then it hit him. Did they know Isabel was Spanish? She smiled at him, unconcerned.

Prince Huzco spoke the strange words of the Quechua language in a booming voice as Juan translated. "The people of Karu Orq'o welcome our honored guests. We look upon them with great happiness and gratitude. They saved the sacred treasures of Inti. We thank them and invite them to a special celebration!" The crowd cheered as Prince Huzco nodded his head.

Lantic indicated the guests should walk up the steps. T'ika ran ahead calling, *"Chatu, K'ak'a!"*

Pedro explained, "K'ak'a means uncle."

"Good thing they don't know what it means in English," Josh whispered to Martin.

When the visitors neared the top, Dr. Wells bowed. Martin followed suit and looked up into the dark, solemn eyes of Prince Huzco. He found only kindness, nothing to fear.

The group sat along the stones below Prince Huzco and Chatu. Martin stared at the sundial, a huge stone pillar with a rounded top that towered above the left side of the plaza. As the noon Sun erased all shadows, Prince Huzco declared, "Inti sits upon his throne. Let the celebration begin!"

"Hey, a parade!" Josh pointed to a long procession of guards followed by men playing wooden flutes and metal gongs. Women trailed behind the musicians with silver trays.

Martin thought he recognized the cup they had examined from Dr. Leonard's bag of loot. "Dr. Wells, those must be the stolen things."

Dr. Wells nodded his head in agreement. At least twenty-five women carried the priceless pieces—a beautifully tooled gold bowl, a silver goblet studded with red stones, a small statue of a llama and a mask of Inti.

One after another, they marched around the plaza and assembled in two lines on the far side. The men began to play lively music. Dancers appeared wearing colorful feathers and waving woven ribbons in the air. They spun with light, graceful steps.

Isabel kept poking her elbow into Martin's ribs, "Can you believe it!"

Martin could barely believe it, but he wished she'd stop. His ribs hurt.

When the entertainment finished, Juan explained, "Next, we go to the Temple of the Sun to return the stolen items and give thanks to Inti. We'll follow after Prince Huzco and Chatu."

Guards marched to the throne, followed by four men carrying a flat seat draped in red and gold cloth. Prince Huzco and Chatu walked regally down the stairs and climbed onto the seat. The guests followed behind them.

Isabel squeezed Martin's arm, "I feel like I'm in a dream."

"Yeah, like being in a movie," Martin agreed.

"Maybe when people find out about this, someone will make a movie," Josh said.

"And we can star in it," Martin answered.

Isabel shook her head. "In your dreams."

Prince Huzco and Chatu dismounted and led them into the Temple of the Sun. The temple extended deep into the mountain, a vast cavern with high ceilings and a series of rooms divided by low walls. Dozens of torches burned to illuminate the dark recesses. As Martin's eyes adjusted to the light, he realized the walls were lined with sheets of gold.

Dr. Wells gasped, "Goodness! Truly remarkable."

"Look!" Josh said, pointing to dozens of small shelves carved into the rock, "the *huacas*." They had read "huaca" meant a holy place where small gifts were offered to the gods. Many of the stolen pieces had come from the huacas.

José explained that the painting covering the far wall represented the universe. A golden oval in the center was Viracocha, the invisible parent of the Sun and Moon. Underneath, on either side, a gold Sun and silver Moon hovered above their children, the Morning and Evening Stars and, below them, the Earth and Water.

They reached the steps to the main altar at the far end of the temple. Gold and silver pots and figures surrounded a giant

gold Inti. Prince Huzco got on his knees and everyone followed. Lantic spoke as men and women slowly placed the stolen items on the altar, bowing low over and over before Inti.

No one tried to translate, but Martin guessed it must be something about giving thanks. It went on and on until Martin's knees ached. He didn't know how much longer he could stand it. Josh made a face at him, and Martin had to turn away quickly, afraid he would start laughing. At last Lantic finished, and they rose.

As they left the temple and walked once more into the blinding sunlight, Martin tripped over a step and nearly fell.

Isabel grabbed his elbow to steady him. "Your shoelace is untied."

"Thanks," Martin replied. Those darn nylon shoelaces were always coming undone. He crouched on the ground to tie them.

In the blink of an eye, six guards surrounded him, their spears pointed toward his heart, their faces iron masks. Martin gasped for air.

Chapter 22

The Feast

MARTIN TRIED TO put his hands up, but his body had frozen with fear.

Juan spoke rapidly in Quechua, followed by the stern voice of Prince Huzco. The soldiers stepped back and lowered their spears but still glared at Martin.

"I was tying my shoes," Martin managed in a hoarse whisper.

"You surprised the guards," Juan explained.

It struck Martin that they had been speaking in Spanish all day, and he had understood everything. At the moment though, it didn't seem important.

"Can you tell them I'm sorry?" Martin tried to smile at the guards, but his mouth was so dry he felt his lips stick to his teeth. He imagined he looked more like a grinning chimpanzee.

Prince Huzco stepped forward and waved the guards away. He leaned over to study the sneakers as Martin quickly double knotted his laces. Prince Huzco grinned and nodded in approval. Relief flooded over Martin as he stood on shaky legs.

The guards continued to stare at him with wary eyes. He could understand how they would be afraid of strangers who showed up out of nowhere. After all, they hadn't had very good luck with foreigners in the past.

"Prince Huzco will show you the Golden Garden," Juan said and ushered the group along. They stepped into an area next to the temple where pools of cool water intertwined with rock-lined dirt paths. Gold and silver statues of snakes, llamas, rabbits, wild pigs, corn, flowers, and Sun masks stood out everywhere on the dirt floor of the garden.

"This is weird," Martin whispered to Isabel.

"Simply astounding," Dr. Wells muttered. "What a day!"

Isabel stroked the head of a golden llama, smiling, "Quite a zoo."

"Boy, am I hungry!" Josh moaned. "I hope we eat soon."

*   *   *

The feast took place in a rectangular hall built of wood with a thatched straw roof. Light streamed through doorways at both ends, and a cool breeze flowed across five-foot openings along the tops of the walls. Straw mats covered the dirt floor, and woven rugs were laid in a circle as seats for the prince and his guests. A silver plate and bowl waited in front of each place.

Martin settled with the other kids on one side of the eating area, sitting cross-legged next to Isabel and Pedro. Chatu smiled broadly at them. Soon a procession of women arrived with trays of roasted pork, guinea fowl and other meats. Martin wasn't sure he wanted to know what they all were. Another line of servers bore bowls of stew made with corn, beans, potatoes and other vegetables. Steam rose off the bowls, sending delicious scents wafting through the room.

"I could eat a whole pig; I'm so hungry," Josh said, eyeing the brimming platters.

Isabel frowned at Josh. "Don't forget, Dr. Wells told us to use our best manners."

"I know," Josh huffed.

Once the dishes had been placed in the center, Prince Huzco bowed his head at his guests and spread his hands indicating they should enjoy the food. Juan explained the food had been prepared in their honor and blessed by the priests in the name of Inti. Chatu was the first to reach out and take a portion of pork. He ate with his fingers.

"Pedro, what are these for?" Martin asked, holding up a funny-looking wooden instrument resembling a spoon, only the recessed portion was long and narrow.

Pedro smiled and demonstrated, using the implement to scoop stew into his silver bowl. "Like this," he said.

Isabel tried some of the stew. "This tastes like the food we had at the festival."

Juan nodded his head across the way. "Our traditions and food are very old. Things do not change."

The women servers returned with silver goblets for each person.

Josh peered in his glass. "What's this?"

"It's chicha, the corn drink," Pedro answered.

Corn beer is more like it, Martin thought. He whispered to Isabel, "It smells nasty."

By this time, Dr. Wells had sipped his drink. He leaned over discreetly. "Sorry, children, I can't allow you to drink this. Your parents will not be happy with me if I bring you back tipsy."

Martin remembered the festival and how the adults had gotten louder and wilder as the evening wore on. "That's okay. I don't think I'd like it, anyway." However, he noticed Pedro, Chatu and T'ika drank the chicha and seemed to like it a lot.

Just when Martin thought he couldn't eat another bite, new plates arrived piled with berries, bananas and mangos from the jungle and sweet corn cakes.

Finally Chatu asked Prince Huzco if he could introduce them to some other young people. Prince Huzco excused them, and they left the adults deep in conversation. At least thirty kids waited outside the doorway. Chatu and T'ika introduced Martin, Isabel and Josh to the eager faces. Soon Pedro could hardly keep up with the translations. The Inca children crowded around, touching the strangers' clothes and shoes.

"I feel like some kind of alien," Martin said.

Isabel laughed, "I guess for them, we might as well be from another planet."

Josh grinned as a little girl untied his shoelaces and smiled with delight. "Enjoy being celebrities for a day," he said. "No one's ever paid this much attention to me."

As the afternoon Sun faded, Dr. Wells gathered the group for the return trip. "I hate to end this wonderful day, but we must start back."

A long round of goodbyes ensued before they wound their way through the tunnels and followed the jungle path to Jalca and camp.

At dinner that night, the other team members listened, fascinated by every detail of the visit.

"The food was really good. I ate so much I could hardly stand up," Josh said as his mom shook her head, and his dad laughed.

"And what about Prince

Huzco?" Dr. García asked Dr. Wells. "What was he like?"

"I had a long chat with Prince Huzco, a very wise man." Dr. Wells mopped his brow with a handkerchief. "He has consulted the priests and prayed to Inti to guide him in his decisions. He realizes life will change in Karu Orq'o, that people must be free to choose their own lives."

"What does he think about the minister of the interior's visit?" Dr. Arturo asked anxiously.

"He is looking forward to meeting him. I told him there are many ways to protect Karu Orq'o. The Island of Ni'ihua in Hawaii is an excellent model."

"What's that?" Isabel asked.

"An island in Hawaii where only native Hawaiians live and no visitors are permitted. They continue to live as the Hawaiian people have lived traditionally. I guess you would call it a cultural preserve," Dr. Wells explained.

"But you mean we'd never get to go back again?" Martin sat up alarmed.

"I should think special friends would be allowed to visit occasionally," Dr. Wells assured him.

"Did you broach the subject of studying Karu Orq'o?" Dr. García asked.

"That's the best news. I'd have to say Prince Huzco and I rather got on. He isn't opposed to the idea of documenting life in Karu Orq'o. He's willing to discuss it with the minister next week."

Isabel turned to Martin with uncertain eyes. He knew what she was thinking, the unspoken questions everyone shared. What did this mean for the excavation team? Would they be staying, or would some of them soon be going home? Martin didn't know what he hoped for anymore.

Chapter 23

Saying Goodbye

MARTIN PAUSED AT the computer, contemplating his last words to Charlie from Jalca, before heading home. Home! He couldn't believe they were really going home. The past six months in Peru had felt more like two years, so much had happened.

He looked up as Isabel poked her head in the door. "What're you doing?"

"I'm sending a couple of e-mails."

"I guess we're really leaving tomorrow." She gave a crooked smile. "Jenny's out there crying in Paolo's arms."

Martin rolled his eyes and shook his head. "She always makes such a big deal out of everything. I don't know what her problem is. My parents already said she can visit the Bertollis this summer."

Isabel looked wistfully at Martin, "I wish we could have stayed longer."

"I know," Martin leaned over with his elbows on his knees. "But at least we got to stay to uncover the temple, or we would've gone home months ago."

Prince Huzco had agreed that the excavation team could complete their work unearthing the buried side of the temple.

With the help of the village men, work had moved quickly. During these months, team members were allowed to visit Karu Orq'o. Only Dr. and Mrs. Wells, Dr. Arturo and Sara Bassett would remain behind to document life in the Inca city.

"It's not as good as staying the whole year," Isabel's lips formed a pout.

"I'm excited to get home, but I'll miss—well, you know, everything." He shrugged and studied the wooden floor, unable to look in her eyes. Who would have guessed his best friend in Peru would be a girl? But he liked everything about Isabel, her sense of adventure, the way nothing seemed to scare her, even her teasing about the way he spoke Spanish. It was hard to pinpoint, but there was something different about her, different from being friends with Charlie or Ryan. He couldn't quite explain what he'd been feeling for weeks now, as he lay in bed at night. His heart was heavy at the thought of leaving. He

couldn't tell her how much he'd miss her, how much he liked her.

He brightened. "It's going to be so tight when you visit this summer. I can't wait for you to meet Charlie and Trevor and Ryan."

"I'll be one of the guys again." She laughed and looked back outside for a moment. "Did your parents go to the signing ceremony?"

"Yeah. And your mom?"

She nodded yes.

Over the past several months, Prince Huzco and the minister of the interior had worked out an agreement for the future of Karu Orq'o. The Peruvian government agreed to recognize the city as a protected state where Prince Huzco, Chatu and their successors would maintain rule. The outside world would be kept at bay—for now. This afternoon was the formal signing of the agreement, and most of the adults had gone to Karu Orq'o for the ceremony.

After a long silence, Martin asked, "What's Josh up to?"

"Oh, I forgot. That's why I was looking for you." She tossed her long waves over her shoulder. "Josh wants to take a last walk down the path."

"Okay, I'll be done in a minute."

"Bring your skateboard. I'm going to trade off with Josh on my scooter."

*   *   *

Martin sat next to Isabel in the airport terminal, running his miniature skateboard down the chair's arm. The Bertollis and Wilsons had left that morning. Martin's flight departed next.

"You have my address," Isabel said. "Is it in a safe place? I mean, you won't lose it, will you?"

"Of course not. I put it in my pocket." Martin pulled out a crumpled piece of paper. "Besides, Mom has it too. She won't lose it."

"We sure had an amazing time." Isabel looked at him with her big, green eyes.

"Yeah. No one at home will believe what happened." Martin glanced at his sister wiping her eyes with a tissue. She had been crying on and off ever since Paolo had left. He hoped Isabel wasn't going to cry.

"I can't wait to visit." Isabel tugged at her llama belt. "It's only three months away," she added cheerfully.

Martin's dad turned toward them and gathered up the bags. "Well, Son, we better get to our gate. Isabel, we'll miss you."

Martin stood awkwardly as Dr. García planted quick kisses on both his cheeks and Isabel hugged his parents. Jenny joined in, sniffling the whole time.

Isabel turned to Martin and whispered, "I'll miss you."

Martin looked down and studied his shoes. "Yeah, I know what you mean."

Suddenly she leaned forward and gave him a quick kiss on the cheek.

His cheeks grew hot. "'Bye," he said, shuffling away.

"Carmen, be sure to write," Mom said.

As they approached the security checkpoint, Martin turned around one last time to find Isabel still watching and wiping her cheek with the back of her hand.

"Hey, don't forget your scooter," he called out. "I know some really tight places to ride. Maybe we'll find another secret path."

**Elaine Russell's** readers will appreciate the detailed research that created a lively cultural environment in *Martin McMillan and the Lost Inca City*. The author majored in history at the University of California, Davis and received a masters in economics from California State University, Sacramento. From there she launched a career as a resource economist and environmental consultant which has led to extensive experience in public speaking, to accompany her skill as a writer.

Ask for Polar Bear & Company's quality paperback books at your local book store. Archival, recycled paper. Distributed by Biblio/NBN: 1-800-462-6420.

A Voice for the Redwoods, by Loretta Halter, an elementary school teacher, takes us into the world of the redwood trees by focusing on the life of one tree. The author conveys the sense of time that it takes to grow a redwood by following its life from seedling to adult. We meet Native Americans, from generation to generation, then early loggers and people of our time. An ideal book for the classroom. Endorsed by Earth First! and by Fmr. US Rep. Dan Hamburg, Executive Director for Voice of the Environment.
    33 b&w illustrations and scientific drawings, ISBN 1-882190-66-1, 9 1/4 x 6 1/8", 64pp, $14.

Madalynn the Monarch Butterfly and Her Quest to Michoacan, by Mary Baca Haque. Journey with Madalynn, a unique monarch butterfly, as she migrates to Mexico. Madalynn has a bright, energetic, liberating spirit that keeps her focused on her quest. She encounters a variety of birds on her travels that entertain and educate. A Spanish translation and a study guide makes it an ideal tool for educators and schools. Foreword by Guillermo Castilleja, Vice President of WWF of Latin America. With a Spanish Translation by Francisco Lancaster-Jones, professor at the graduate program of Translation and Interpretation at the Universidad Autónoma de Guadalajara.
    27 b&w Illustrations with bird species, ISBN 1-882190-52-1, 9 1/4 x 6 1/8", 64 pages, $14.

Manitou, A Mythological Journey in Time, by Ramona du Houx. Join in comical performances and musical excursions with Apollo, Venus, Mother Earth, and other mythological figures from around the world. Uncover amazing mysteries experiencing nature. "A book declaring that love and freedom are things worth striving for... perhaps that is the message young people are listening for. They can find it in a place called Manitou." —Judy Harrison, The Bangor Daily News.
            Novel, 13 b&w illustrations, ISBN 1-882190-77-7, 7 x 4 1/2", 224pp, $12.

Millicent the Magnificent, by Burton Hoffmann. Amanda discovers that there is magic in music when a mockingbird she names "Millicent" speaks. When Millicent sings, Amanda's piano teacher is enchanted, and the new friends and family plan a musical career for the magical mockingbird. "Millicent is a charming story that will help children appreciate the wonders of classical music." —John Brown, The Eagle Review
            7 b&w illustrations, ISBN 1-882190-68-8, 8 1/5 x 5 1/5, 64 pages, $12.

Women Who Walk with the Sky, by Dawn Levesque. "It is fun for children of this age to wrap their minds around stories where the worlds of nature, magic, and ordinary people meet. . . . *Women Who Walk with the Sky* is particularly well written for reading aloud. The tales are short and the writing flows with images. In addition, the stories lend themselves well to discussion and . . . may just strike the imagination of the writers and dreamers in your classroom." —Cindy Clevenger, The National Monetssori Reporter.
"It's great to finally have a children's Native American mythology with triumphant female heroines who, in the course of their adventures . . . explore the natural world." —Maine in Print
            34 b&w illustrations, ISBN 1-882190-12-2, 9 1/4 x 6 1/8", 64pp, $14.